Milo March is a hard-dri  James-Bondian character. H
combination of personality, bi   ...ce, and intellect. He is a shrewd   ...character, a crack shot, and a deeper character than I have found in most of the other spy/thriller novels I've read. But, above all, he is a con-man—and a very good one. It is Milo March himself who makes the series worth reading.

—Don Miller, *The Mystery Nook* fanzine 12

Steeger Books is proud to reissue twenty-three vintage novels and stories by M.E. Chaber, whose Milo March Mysteries deliver mile-a-minute action and breezily readable entertainment for thriller buffs.

Milo is an Insurance Investigator who takes on the tough cases. Organized crime, grand theft, arson, suspicious disappearances, murders, and millions and millions of dollars—whatever it is, Milo is just the man for the job. Or even the only man for it.

During World War II, Milo was assigned to the OSS and later the CIA. Now in the Army Reserves, with the rank of Major, he is recalled for special jobs behind the Iron Curtain. As an agent, he chops necks, trusses men like chickens to steal their uniforms, shoots point blank at secret police—yet shows compassion to an agent from the other side.

Whatever Milo does, he knows how to do it right. When the work is completed, he returns to his favorite things: women, booze, and good food, more or less in that order....

THE MILO MARCH MYSTERIES

Hangman's Harvest

No Grave for March

The Man Inside

As Old as Cain

The Splintered Man

A Lonely Walk

The Gallows Garden

A Hearse of Another Color

So Dead the Rose

Jade for a Lady

Softly in the Night

Uneasy Lies the Dead

Six Who Ran

Wanted: Dead Men

The Day It Rained Diamonds

A Man in the Middle

Wild Midnight Falls

The Flaming Man

Green Grow the Graves

The Bonded Dead

Born to Be Hanged

Death to the Brides

The Twisted Trap: Six Milo March Stories

The Man Inside

KENDELL FOSTER CROSSEN
Writing as
M.E. CHABER

With an Afterword by
KENDRA CROSSEN BURROUGHS

STEEGER BOOKS / 2020

PUBLISHED BY STEEGER BOOKS
Visit steegerbooks.com for more books like this.

PUBLISHING HISTORY

Magazine
"The Man Inside," *Bluebook*, vol. 98, no. 2 (December 1953). Illustrated by Al Tarter. A condensed version.

Hardcover
New York: Henry Holt & Co. (A Novel of Suspense), February 1954. Dust jacket by Ben Feder, Inc.
Toronto: George J. McLeod, 1954.
London: Eyre & Spottiswoode, 1955.

Paperback
Popular Library #632, as *Now It's My Turn*, 1954. Cover by Ray Johnson.
Popular Library Giant #G282, 1958 reprint. Cover by Ray Johnson.
New York: Paperback Library (63-213), A Milo March Mystery, #4, January 1970. Cover by Robert McGinnis.

Movie
The Man Inside (UK, September 1958). Directed by John Gilling and starring Jack Palance and Anita Ekberg. Screenplay by David Shaw, based on the novel.

ISBN: 978-1-61827-497-7

For Martha

II Samuel 1:26

CONTENTS

INTERLUDE 1

The blue diamond lay by itself in the very center of the velvet-covered table. The light flashed from it, changing with every heartbeat. There were times when it seemed filled with blue fire. Other times—and his breath came faster—when it seemed that he could almost see himself in mysterious minia-ture deep in the flame.

He was hardly aware that a third person had entered the room.

"There's someone on the phone," the secretary said. "He won't speak with anyone else."

The other man glanced at the diamond, but the gesture was brief and cursory. There was no reason to doubt some-one he'd known for fifteen years. He followed the secretary from the room.

He knew when the other man went to answer the telephone, although he didn't take his eyes from the blue diamond. He had planned on that phone call for five years. It was part of something he had planned for twenty years.

He picked up the diamond. Its surface was cool against his warm flesh. He held it for a second, watching the changing light, then dropped it into his pocket. He turned and left the room. There was no one to see him go.

He had rehearsed it so often in his mind that this time felt no different. Although this time it was real. He could feel the diamond in his pocket. He had known from the first that it belonged to him. It had always been his; now he had taken possession of it. That was all.

He walked slowly down the stairs. Twenty-one steps. Then he pushed open the heavy iron door and stepped out into the corridor. He closed the door behind him, smiling at the detective who stood guarding that door. He took his left hand from his pocket, his finger reluctantly leaving the diamond. He plunged his right hand into a pocket, curling it around the cold metal.

"Leaving early today, Mr. Carter?" the detective said.

"No," he answered truthfully. "I'm leaving right on time."

Everything was on time. The phone call had come in right on the second. He'd been right in his estimate of how long it would take Robert Stone to answer the phone. He'd had one second to spare in the time he'd given himself to pocket the diamond and walk down the stairs.

"You're right," he corrected himself gravely. "I am one second early."

The detective laughed.

Here he had allowed himself an extra twenty seconds. He didn't know about alarms; it might have aroused suspicion to have asked. He couldn't be sure how long the telephone conversation would last. So he had added the extra twenty seconds.

He stepped through the outer door to the sidewalk, wondering why the detective laughed.

"Wait a minute," the detective called.

He knew he'd been wise to include that twenty seconds. But it wasn't much time. Not enough to ask any questions or answer any. He turned and stepped back into the small corridor. He took the gun from his pocket, steadied it, and pulled the trigger. It didn't sound as loud as he'd expected. He watched curiously as the detective slumped to the floor. He had never seen anyone die before.

He returned the gun to his pocket and stepped back out on the street. He glanced at his watch. He was surprised to see that it hadn't taken twenty seconds.

He walked briskly to the corner. Nobody noticed him. They never had.

ONE

Did you ever walk through Skid Row—the Skid Row of any city—and see an old woman, blowsy with fat, passed out with a Tokay smile on her face? Did you ever stop to look at her and wonder what the smile meant? Maybe, you thought, she was dreaming about the time when she was a young chippy. Well, that's how New York City looks when you fly over her early in the morning—a great, sprawling, old woman of a city. You rub the sleep out of your eyes and look at her with mixed feelings; equal parts of sympathy, sadness, envy, and disgust.

It was Saturday morning. The plane came down at LaGuardia on time. I had slept on the plane the night before, but it hadn't been enough. I had the false sense of well-being that comes from too little sleep.

As I came into the terminal the loudspeaker was blasting: "Mr. Milo March. Will you please go to the Pan American Airways counter. Mr. Milo March …"

I walked across the terminal to where I could see the Pan American sign. There were three men beside the counter. One of them was leaning on it. He looked about forty-five. He had all the earmarks of a cop, except that his suit had cost more than the average cop could afford. Anywhere I would have guessed he was a cop who had resigned to take a better job.

His past was written in the way he stood, the way his gaze swept over the terminal.

I walked over to him. "You're John Franklin," I said before he could know I wasn't just walking by.

He looked at me and knew I was showing off. But he liked it.

"Milo March," he said and we shook hands. He glanced at the counter and the other two men. "I thought it would be easier to have you paged since we'd never met. How'd you make me?"

"Easy," I said. "Those two are citizens. You've got ex-cop written all over you. And I know the Great Northern Insurance Company. They like to get their money's worth. They'd buy an ex-cop to head their investigation department."

"I was on the New York force for twenty years," he said, "so I guess it might show. But how'd you figure the ex?"

"The suit. It's too expensive even for a cop with his hand out. He'd be investigated ten minutes after he showed in it."

He laughed. "You'd probably like some breakfast. We'll pick up your luggage afterward."

We went into the restaurant. I ordered breakfast and he had coffee. He waited until I'd finished my eggs.

"You've got about twenty-four hours to cover the background," he said. "You want to go around by yourself, or you want me to tag along?"

"If it won't hurt your feelings, I'll do it alone," I said. I lit a cigarette and went to work on the coffee. "Why only twenty-four hours?"

"Then you're getting on another plane. If you don't catch

the one tomorrow, you'll have to wait until Wednesday. That would put you a week behind your man."

I nodded. "I don't know anything about this," I told him. "I was just starting myself a big evening last night when the head of Trans-World Insurance called, telling me to come to New York and see John Franklin of Great Northern. He told me it was a big case, but he says that even when it's a string of cultured pearls insured for ten bucks."

He laughed. "This time he's right. It's a diamond."

"One diamond?"

"One diamond," he said dryly. "We insured it five years ago for seven hundred thousand dollars."

That's a lot of money even in a Republican administration. I tried to show my respect, but my eyebrows wouldn't go high enough. "Why me?" I asked. "Great Northern must have offices full of investigators right here in New York. Why import one from Denver?"

He pulled some money from his pocket and paid the check. "Sure," he said. "We've got investigators. Good ones, too. I hired them myself. They crack most of the cases we get. But they're not fancy. On the other hand, we've had some real tough cases out around Denver that were cleaned up with the kind of flourish an old cop appreciates. This is a special case. It needs someone with more imagination than Great Northern has—including me."

One way you looked at it, it was flattering. But another way, it only meant I was going to have to work to live up to what he thought I was. "How special?" I asked.

We left the restaurant. "Our boys," he said, "know the habits of most of the icemen working today. They can look over a job and tell you who pulled it. And they'll know how to go about finding him. But this one was pulled by an amateur. This was his one job. He probably doesn't want to pull another one. There's good reason to believe he'll never try to sell this diamond. And there are other angles you'll learn as you go along—including murder."

"That ought to put it in the laps of the regular cops," I said.

"It does," he said. "But as I said, this one needs imagination. More than they have. I'm not selling the New York department short; it's one of the best forces in the world. But this one is over their heads, as you'll see."

We stopped off and picked up my luggage. Then we went out to the parking lot and climbed into his car. He didn't say any more until we turned in to a parkway and headed for the city.

"Here's an outline," he said. "I won't fill in any of the details. I'd rather you got those from each of the sources. You ever hear of the House of Stones?"

I had. A guy named Robert Stone who was one of the biggest individual operators in valuable jewels. I said as much.

"He's that," John Franklin said. "He deals in everything from twenty-five-dollar engagement rings to the biggest. Has an old brownstone house in the fifties. He's a smart dealer, but he's also a man who loves good stones. They say he's refused to sell one that he liked. You'll see him first."

"He's the victim?" I asked.

"Depends on how you look at it," he said with a grin. "Our stockholders will probably think we're the victims. But he had the diamond. He doesn't have it now. He had a regular customer. A little accountant who kept saving his money and buying diamonds. The little guy liked diamonds—especially the ones he couldn't afford. Every week he stopped in at the House of Stones. Sometimes he bought. Sometimes he didn't. But every week Robert Stone brought out prize jewels to show him. There was one particular diamond—Stone'll tell you all about it—he'd looked at it every week for the past five years. Two hundred and sixty times. But yesterday, while he was looking at it, Stone was called to the phone. The little accountant walked out with the diamond."

"The murder?" I asked.

"The detective who guarded the front door. Private detective. That one's funny, too. The cops will tell you about it."

"You've got an idea where he is?"

He shook his head. "We know where he went—although we only discovered that yesterday, and it happened Wednesday. But we don't know where he is. I've got a hunch there's a big difference between where he went and where he is. The Homicide boys think it's going to be easy. I've got a different idea. That's why you're on it."

"Where'd he go?" I asked.

"Lisbon. It's a small place—but from there you can get a plane to almost anywhere. And he'd been there more than a day before we even knew where he'd gone."

"Homicide get in touch with the Policía Internacional e de Defesa donEstado?" I asked.

"State Police?" he asked.

I nodded.

"Where'd you pick up the name?" he asked curiously.

"I was there during part of the war," I said. "OSS. Lisbon was like a convention hall for spies. If you couldn't find a spy anywhere else, you went to Lisbon. You'd usually find him in a café on the Rossio Square listening to a *fado*—one of those sad songs the Portuguese listen to when they feel gay."

He laughed. "We've contacted the local police. Maybe they'll get around to looking for him tomorrow."

"They're slow," I admitted, "except when somebody's gunning for their dictator. But don't be fooled by the fact they don't rush around like New York cops. They still get results."

"Probably," he grunted. "But I'd like to make a bet. I'll bet that nobody finds him in Lisbon—not even you."

"Oh well," I said, settling down in the seat. "I've always wanted to go around the world on an expense account."

He laughed without humor and turned his attention to his driving. He obviously didn't intend to talk anymore. That suited me. I relaxed and pretended I didn't have a care in the world.

He didn't say any more until he brought the car to a stop in front of an old brownstone building in the east fifties. "This is it," he said. "The House of Stones. Robert Stone is expecting you. When you've finished with him, go over and see Captain Jim Gregory at the Nineteenth Precinct. He'll be expecting you, too. You can also see the Homicide captain if you like, but Jim will have all the dope and he'll give you more time. He'll have the list of everyone else you'll want to see."

"Then?" I asked.

"Come back to Great Northern before closing time. We'll

have a doctor there to give you all the shots you may need. You've got a passport, haven't you?"

I nodded. "It was renewed about six months ago. But I don't need a visa for Portugal."

"You may need one later," he said. "Well, it's your ball, Milo."

"I thought it was," I said dryly. "I caught a glimpse of the figure eight on it." I opened the door and got out on the sidewalk. "I'll see you."

He nodded and drove away. I turned and went into the building. The ground floor of the old brownstone had been remodeled so that there was an outer door, then a short corridor, and finally a big door that looked as if it was made of solid steel. There was a guy standing beside the inner door. He looked like a cop. A nervous cop.

"Yes?" he asked. He tried to make it sound polite, but it came out more like a challenge.

"I want to see Mr. Stone," I told him. "I'm Milo March. From the insurance company."

He looked relieved. "He's expecting you," he said. "Just a minute." He turned around and used a phone on the wall. All he did was announce my name. A moment later there was a buzzing sound and he swung the door open.

I went up the stairs. A well-dressed middle-aged woman was waiting at the head of the stairs for me.

"Mr. March?" she asked.

I nodded.

"This way, please."

I followed her. We went through what seemed to be a

display room. Everything was expensive and in good taste. There was a small table in the center of the room. The top of it was covered with black velvet. A small spotlight was set in the ceiling and trained on the tabletop.

She knocked lightly on the next door and then opened it. She stood to one side for me to go in. "Mr. March, Mr. Stone," she said.

He stood up behind his desk and we looked at each other. He was probably about fifty. Well dressed. A little gray in his hair. A little heavy, but it looked good on him. A rather handsome face, deeply tanned and unlined. He didn't look like a man who had just lost seven hundred thousand dollars.

He held out his hand and we shook. I told him what I'd been thinking. He smiled.

"I haven't lost seven hundred thousand dollars," he said. "The insurance company will give me the money. What I have lost is a diamond which can't be replaced. No amount of money can do that."

I sat down in the chair in front of his desk. "Tell me about it."

He smiled again. "I've already told it so many times, I feel I could repeat it in my sleep. You want to hear about the diamond or the man?"

"Both," I said. "All I have are the bare outlines. I could read most of it in reports, but I'd rather hear you tell it."

He nodded patiently. "The diamond first?"

"If that's the way you want to tell it."

He leaned back and got a distant look in his eyes. "Mr. March, did you ever hear of the Tavernier Blue?"

"No."

"It was a diamond," he said. His voice had grown soft, the way some men's voices will when they speak of a woman. "A blue diamond. One hundred and twelve carats. A man named Jean-Baptiste Tavernier brought it from India to France in 1642.* Twenty-six years later, in 1668, it was sold to Louis XIV. During the French Revolution, the diamond disappeared. There have been many theories concerning what happened to it. The most popular one—which we now know to be mostly true—is that it was cut after being stolen and the cutter blundered—so the Blue broke in two. The Hope Diamond appeared in London in 1830, when it was purchased by Henry Hope. I believe it was the smaller part of the Blue. The larger half seemed to be lost forever—until 1946."

"Your diamond was the other half?" I asked.**

"Yes. I called it by the original name. The Tavernier Blue. Sixty-seven carats of blue flame. When the war was over, it was discovered among the possessions of Adolf Hitler. With it was a complete history of the stone from the day it disappeared. This, of course, made it still more valuable."

"How big?" I asked.

He showed me with his hands. It must have been only a little smaller than a golf ball.

"And it's really worth seven hundred thousand?" I asked.***

---

* For more on the Tavernier Blue, see the Afterword. (All footnotes were added by the editor.)
** There is no evidence that the real Tavernier Blue accidentally broke in half, so this aspect of the story is fictional.
*** An inflation calculator equates US $700,000 in 1954 to over $6.5 million in 2018.

"The value of a stone," he said, "is determined by what someone is willing to pay for it. This one was established because shortly after I bought it, I refused an offer of seven hundred thousand. As I mentioned, the history of the stone undoubtedly increases its value. You know, Mr. March, for a long time the Hope Diamond was considered a bad-luck stone. That could more accurately be said of the Tavernier Blue. During the past three hundred years it changed hands fifty-seven times. Only five times was it legitimately bought and sold. Thirty-eight persons were murdered in the process of changing ownership. And poor Mike was the thirty-ninth."

"The guard?" I asked.

He nodded.

"Why hadn't you sold the diamond?" I asked. "Holding out for a bigger price?"

"No. There was enough profit in the offer." He hesitated. "Mr. March, have you seen many valuable stones?"

"Not recently," I said dryly. "My income doesn't run to such things."

"Income has little to do with what I'm talking about," he said. "Forty years ago a man fell in love with the statue of Nefertiti in the Egyptian Museum of Berlin. He couldn't rest until he'd stolen her. Not to sell, remember, but only that he might have her in his room to look at every day. Some men are like that about rare stones. I am myself. I could spend hours every day looking at the Tavernier Blue. It is a diamond with a real personality—one that changes every minute even as you look at it. Sometimes I had the feeling that it was the diamond that owned me, instead of the other way around. That's why I understand Carter so well."

"Who's Carter?" I asked.

He looked surprised. "The man who took the Tavernier Blue," he said.

"Tell me about him."

"His full name is Samson Hercules Carter. I guess that represented his father's wishful thinking. Carter's only about five feet six and never weighed over a hundred and thirty pounds. I had a feeling he resented the name, although he never said anything."

"Can't blame him for that," I said.

He nodded. "Carter first came here fifteen or sixteen years ago. He'd been coming here for a year or more, buying small diamonds—he spent about two thousand dollars every year that I knew him—before I met him. After that I waited on him myself, for Samson Carter was a man who also loved rare gems. He'd come in every week, although he didn't buy every time he came, and I'd show him other things I had. Diamonds, emeralds, rubies, sapphires, he loved them all. We'd sit at the table in the next room and look at the stones. Sometimes for an hour, if I wasn't too busy. Then I got the Tavernier Blue."

"He liked that, huh?"

"The best." He looked at me sharply. "Don't misunderstand, March. I felt the same way about the Blue. In a way it was a bond between Carter and me—our only bond, but the sort that can exist between two people who are attracted to the same thing. After that, when he came up, I always brought out the diamond. He didn't have to ask. I knew how he felt.

He'd fallen in love with the diamond—something a lot of other men had done in the past three hundred years."

"What happened Wednesday?" I asked.

"He came as he always did. He bought a small diamond for a hundred dollars, and then I brought out the Tavernier Blue. He obviously didn't feel like talking and I naturally respected his desire. He'd been here about fifteen minutes when I was called to the phone. I was out of the room about five minutes, and when I returned he was gone."

"Wasn't it unusual to leave someone alone with a diamond worth that much money?"

He grinned wryly. "One of the officials of your company hinted that they might contest the claim on the grounds that I contributed to the theft with my own negligence," he said. "Still, I don't think it was unusual. I had known Carter for fifteen years. I had left him alone with valuable stones before. There was a guard downstairs."

I shrugged. That, after all, was the insurance company's problem. I had asked only out of curiosity. "Can you give me a complete description of the diamond?" I asked, changing the subject.

"I can do better," he said. He opened a drawer and removed something. "Here is a color picture of the Tavernier Blue. There's a description on the back."

It didn't look quite as good as a stack of seven hundred thousand one-dollar bills, but I could see why someone might want to put it in his pocket and take a walk. It was a deep blue, shot through with streaks of light. There was something almost hypnotic about it, even in a photograph. I slipped it in my pocket.

"I guess that's about all you can give me," I said. I stood up. "Sorry to have taken up your time, Mr. Stone."

"There is one more thing," he said. He seemed to be looking for something as he stared into my eyes. "I tried to tell this to the police, but it is beyond their comprehension. You seem intelligent, and Mr. Franklin says that you have imagination. There is one thing you must understand if you are to recover my diamond for me."

He paused and I waited. There was no point in rushing him.

"Samson Carter," he said, "is not a jewel thief. He has stolen one jewel, which is not the same thing. He will not try to sell the Tavernier Blue, and it will be a waste of time trying to catch him from that angle. He probably has enough money— my records show that he owns small diamonds worth thirty thousand dollars—but that isn't the reason. Even if he is starving, Carter will neither sell the diamond nor pawn it. With Carter it is a matter of love. He stole my diamond as another man might try to steal my wife. Unless you understand this, you will never find him."

"What can a diamond do for you on a cold night?" I asked. "Never mind answering that. I wouldn't believe it. But I'll believe what you say about Carter. I'll look for him under a bright moon instead of three brass balls."

As I left, he took a couple of diamonds from a desk drawer and began playing with them absentmindedly. I guessed they weren't very important diamonds—no bigger than a couple of hickory nuts. He was playing with them the way a boy will play with marbles when there's something else on his mind. I shook my head and left for a less rarified atmosphere.

TWO

The Nineteenth Precinct was also on the East Side, only a few blocks from the House of Stones. It was sandwiched in between two fancy districts, but it looked and smelled like every station house in the country. The desk sergeant who looked up as I entered was the bored counterpart of those in a thousand other precincts. Desk sergeants are a special breed. They've listened to so much that everything they hear is just another item for the squeal book.

I told him who I was and who I wanted to see. He flagged down a passing patrolman and told him to show me Captain Gregory's office. He showed me. I knocked on the door and a gruff voice told me to come in.

One look at the Captain told you his whole history. He'd come up the hard way from pounding a beat and it was written all over him. He'd probably been sitting at a desk for ten years or more, but he still looked as if he had tired feet. Sometimes that kind makes the best police official. Usually they're not very smart, but they make up for it by being honest.

I told him who I was and he looked me over with a pair of clear blue eyes that seemed at least fifteen years younger than his sixty years.

"Insurance detective," he said. There was no malice in his

voice, but he made it sound like the tag of a dirty joke. "A fancy kind of private dick. Playing cops."

I grinned at him. "I feel the same way about cops," I told him. "Only I'm broad-minded about it. Some of my best friends are cops."

He grinned back at me. "John said you wouldn't take any of my lip," he said. He leaned back in his chain. "John Franklin and I used to walk a beat together. He's done all right. Sometimes I think I ought to've taken a job like that."

"You wouldn't have liked it," I said. "They would have shoved a padded chair under your behind and taken away your cheap cigars, and you would have died by fifty."

"Maybe you're right," he grunted. You could see that he liked to talk about the things he could have done, but that he wouldn't be any place except where he was. "What can I do for you, March?"

"The works," I said. I took the other chair in the office and got out a cigarette. "How come you're still in on it if it's homicide?"

He chuckled. "You know what they call this section, boy? The Gold Coast. Covered by the Seventeenth and Nineteenth Precincts. The men who live here have bank accounts that are too big, and their women are too fancy and don't have enough to do. So the men load their women down with jewels and the women wear them. That leads to six or seven of every ten cases that come in here. Most of my boys eat, drink, and sleep jewels. You might say they're specialists in jewel thieves. So when there's a killing in connection with jewels, the Homicide boys get bighearted and let us work with them."

"You do the work and they solve the case," I said.

"Something like that," he said. "You been down to see Lieutenant Sanderson or Captain O'Hanlon in Homicide?"

I shook my head. "John Franklin said it would be better if I came to you."

He chuckled again. "The Homicide boys don't take kindly to insurance or private detectives messing around in their murders. Not that I exactly blame them."

"Sure," I said. "But I walk real delicate. I never step on toes unless they're shoved right in under me."

"You look like the delicate type," he said dryly. "Maybe I don't like it so much when someone messes around in a case here in my own precinct, but it looks like this one got away. Somebody's got to get him and it might as well be you."

I nodded and waited. It was time to get started on the case; if I stopped feeding him lines, maybe he'd get around to it. He squirmed on his chair, got out a battered cigar, and lit it. He blew a cloud of acrid smoke in my face.

"See this guy Stone?" he asked.

"Yes."

"Guess he told you how it was pulled, then," he said. "The rest ain't too much. Samson Hercules Carter—hell of a name for a little shrimp. Forty-two years old. Five feet six inches tall, weight one hundred and thirty. Dark hair, dark eyes. No identifying marks. Hair parted on the left side. Wears dark gray or dark blue suits, black shoes, white shirts, and dark ties. Unmarried. As near as we can learn, he never even had a girl. No known relatives."

"Photograph?" I asked.

He snorted. "Passport picture in the files of the State Department. Could be any one of a couple thousand guys walking around. Only picture of him we can find. State Department let us make copies of it."

He passed over a small picture. He was right. It wasn't much to go on for identification. Flat lighting had washed out most of his features.

"Carter was an accountant," the Captain went on. "Worked for the same firm for the last twenty-one years. Made a good salary. He was considered a good, reliable man. Never missed a day of work in all that time."

His voice droned on as he continued to pull out the facts without once glancing at the reports. For fifteen years Carter had lived in the same rooming house. He ate most of his meals at the Automat. He bought only the clothes that he needed. He had no friends, neither men nor women, and never went anywhere except to a neighborhood movie once a month. He had one hobby. It was magic, and it hadn't cost much. In addition to the diamonds he had saved almost twenty-two thousand dollars. He had drawn it all out of the bank on Tuesday. On Wednesday, he had stolen the diamond, killed the guard, and taken a plane to Lisbon.

There was no doubt that he had planned the theft. He had gotten his passport two months earlier. He'd had the reservation on the Lisbon plane for three weeks. The Monday before the theft had been the beginning of his annual vacation. On Tuesday he'd taken his luggage to the airport and checked it. According to the Captain, he had taken only essentials with him, but nothing that he'd left behind pointed to his future plans.

"I got a theory," Captain Gregory said. "I think he started planning this whole thing twenty years ago."

"But Stone didn't even have the Tavernier Blue diamond then," I said.

"Maybe he didn't know what diamond he was going to take, but I'll bet he started working it out. For one thing, he started studying Spanish twenty years ago. Until last week he still had one class a week."

It was an interesting theory, but I wasn't accepting or rejecting anything until I had a clearer picture of Carter. I just nodded, and the Captain went on.

The phone call Stone received while he and Carter were looking at the diamond had been part of it, too. There was a man who worked with Carter. His name was George Harder and he was a bit of a practical joker. Carter had told him about his friend the jeweler and persuaded Harder to call and pretend that he wanted to buy some stones. Harder was to call at a certain time, and he did so. The police had kept Harder under arrest for two days; they were convinced that he was innocent of anything but being Carter's dupe.

"He planned it carefully, all right," the Captain said. "He was that kind of man. He did everything according to schedule. He kept a diary of everything he did, even down to the time he ate every meal. He started that twenty years ago too. But he tore out the pages that might have helped on this."

"Then you think the murder was planned too?"

"He probably planned on the murder only if necessary," he said. "We think we know exactly what happened there. In a way, maybe, the murder came out of his careful planning."

"What does that mean?"

"Next to the body of the murdered guard we found an envelope with Carter's name on it. Regular fare ticket and a compartment ticket for Chicago. On a train leaving Penn Station less than an hour after the theft."

I grinned. "So that's why it took you so long to find out he'd gone to Lisbon," I said.

His face turned a deeper red. "Yeah. It was Friday before we thought of checking airlines. We think he'd meant to leave the train tickets somewhere to throw us off—probably in a taxi. We found out that he took a taxi to Penn Station, walked through the station, and then took another taxi to LaGuardia."

That must have taken some digging with someone as inconspicuous as Carter. The cops hadn't produced much, but they'd been working.

"There was no way the guard at Stone's could have known that Carter had stolen a diamond," the Captain said. "We think what happened was this: The train tickets dropped out of Carter's pocket as he left. The guard saw it and probably tried to stop him to tell him about it. That guard had been working there for ten years, so he knew Carter from seeing him every week. But Carter was so keyed up, he must have thought the guard knew what was in his pocket. So he killed him without waiting to see what he wanted."

It sounded reasonable. I filed it away in my mind.

"That's about it," he said. "We know he planned it for a long time. We even got one lucky break. The guy who sold him the gun saw the story in the papers and remembered Carter. He came in to tell us about it. Carter bought the gun five years ago—just two weeks after Stone first showed him this diamond. We know pretty much how Carter did everything. We know he took the plane on Wednesday and landed in Lisbon on Thursday. That's it." He spread his hands.

"Any word from the Portuguese police?" I asked.

"Yeah. Carter landed in Lisbon Thursday and checked in at the Aviz Hotel. He hasn't been seen since. His two suitcases are still in the hotel room. All his clothes are in them, but no diamond."

"The police have the luggage?"

"No. It's still in his room. The hotel claims that Carter said he might go up to Oporto for a few days. There is no record that he did, but the police left his things in the room."

"Okay," I said. "If you'll tell me where to find this George Harder and give me Carter's address, I'll stop bothering you."

He wrote down the two addresses. Then he scribbled a short note and handed it to me. "There's still a cop at the rooming house. Show him this note and he'll let you in. Everything's there."

"Thanks," I said. I held out my hand and he shook it. "I'll send you a postcard from Lisbon."

"There's something else," he said slowly. "I think you ought to know you're going to have competition. Plenty of it."

"What do you mean?"

"Stone tell you his theory? About the guy taking the diamond because he'd fallen in love with it and that he'd never try to sell it?"

I nodded.

"Maybe he's right," the Captain said. "I wouldn't know

about guys like that. I've been here in this precinct for twenty-five years, dealing with jewel thieves, and I never saw one that wouldn't sell what he stole. But I don't think it makes any difference. I don't think he'll live to sell it. Maybe that's why he's vanished from the hotel."

I lit a cigarette and waited for him to tell it his own way.

"Stone made a mistake," he said. "He gave the whole story to the newspapers that same day. Now, if there's anybody who doesn't know there's a little amateur walking around with a seven hundred thousand dollar diamond in his kick, then it must be somebody who's deaf, dumb, and blind and lives in a cave. Every crook in the world is going to be after Carter and that diamond. We're pretty sure that one is after him already."

"Who?"

"Martin Lomer. One of the really big international jewel thieves. A tough customer. He was here in New York and we're certain he was planning a job. We've been watching him. Then this story broke in the papers Wednesday night and Thursday morning. After the Wednesday plane that Carter took, the next plane to Lisbon is the one you're taking tomorrow. But on Thursday, Martin Lomer caught a flight to Paris. It's only a short trip from there back to Lisbon."

"Got anything on Lomer?"

He dug out a picture with a description on the back. "Lomer has a reputation for being able to change his appearance enough to fool some of the cleverest detectives. But that isn't the problem, March. You can't carry the pictures of all the jewel thieves in the world—but you can bet they'll all be after Carter. That diamond's going to draw them like a magnet picks up filings. The story may have been only in American papers, but you can bet by this time the word's spread. Carter's got the diamond, but his life isn't worth a nickel. If they know you're after Carter, yours won't be either."

"There's inflation everywhere," I told him. I thanked him and left.

I took a subway downtown and found the place where Carter had worked. It was a big office-supply company. Harder was a salesman there. I had to wait a few minutes for him.

What the cops had dug up was all right as far as it went. But John Franklin had been right about one thing. This case needed imagination. I knew there was something I had to look for, but I didn't know what it was. If a man like Samson Carter had planned this for fifteen or twenty years—or even for only the five years since he'd bought the gun—then he had planned it farther than Lisbon. Somewhere there had to be a hint to it.

George Harder came out. He was a big, heavyset man, maybe about forty. I told him why I was there and suggested we talk about it over a couple of drinks. He agreed. We went down to a bar and made ourselves comfortable. He had Canadian Club on the rocks and I had a brandy.

One thing was obvious right from the start. George Harder had always had Carter marked down as a jerk. Now the jerk had not only pulled off something big but had suckered Harder into helping him. Harder was wounded and annoyed.

"Never thought the little jerk would take a breath of air without wanting to pay somebody for it," he said. "Can you imagine the little crook fooling everybody all these years?"

"How long did you know him?"

"Fifteen years. That's how long I've been here with this crummy outfit. Samson must've been here six years before I came."

"Samson Hercules Carter," I said musingly. "He must've taken a lot of ribbing on that name."

"Sure," he said. He grinned suddenly. "You know, one time I spent six months finding a girl with the right name so she could phone him and say, 'Samson, this is Delilah.' "

I worked at it and managed to stretch my face into a smile. "How did he take it?"

"I've got to admit the little squirt took it all right," he said. "He told her he was sorry, but he had just been to a barber shop. Then he hung up."

This time I didn't have to work at it. I was thinking I might have liked Samson Carter.

"What about the phone call he had you make?" I asked.

His face clouded up again. "He told me he wanted to play a joke on this friend of his who was a jeweler. I was to call him at the exact time he told me and pretend I wanted to buy an emerald necklace the guy had for sale. I thought maybe the little jerk was finally getting human, and it sounded like a pretty good joke. Who would've thought he was going to mix me up in a thing like that?"

"Look," I said, "I'm trying to pick up everything I can about Carter. What he was like—what he did—things like that. If you worked with him for fifteen years, you ought to be able to tell me a lot."

"A lot there is to tell," he said. "Samson was never late to work, and he didn't take a day off in twenty-one years. He didn't drink. He didn't smoke. He didn't gamble. I don't think he ever went out with a girl. What the hell is a guy like that going to do with seven hundred thousand bucks?"

"Didn't he have any hobbies?" I asked.

"Hobbies? Sure, he did magic tricks. He used to do something he called multiplying golf balls. A big deal. Then he did tricks with thimbles. Thimbles! Yeah, Samson was a big man with thimbles." He laughed loudly at his own joke and had another drink on me.

"If you had to sum Carter up," I said, "would you say he was a methodical man? One who always did everything the same way?"

"That was Samson. Every day exactly the same. To work at the same time. To lunch at the same time. The same thing at night. He even said the same things every day. You suppose he was really spending all his time planning this job?"

"Maybe," I said. I was pushing for something, but I didn't know what it was. "With a guy that methodical, you ought to notice if he did anything unusual."

"Sure, but he never did."

"You're certain?" I asked. "Fifteen years is a long time for a man never to change. Surely there must have been something in that time. Didn't he ever get interested in Surrealist art, the care and feeding of orphans, delinquent veterans of the Civil War, or something?"

"No—" He broke off and something flickered over his face. "Wait a minute, maybe there was something. Let me think a minute." He needed another Canadian Club to help him think. "Let me see, it must have been five years ago. I'd forgotten about it until just now. I wouldn't have known about it except that Samson asked me where the Tombs Prison was. It was so much out of keeping, I decided to trail along and see what happened."

"What did?" I asked when he paused.

"I don't know. Samson went in and saw one of the prisoners. I couldn't go in with him. I asked him about it when he came out and he said that he was interested in some kind of a crime prevention society. That didn't sound right either, but that's all he'd tell me. He said he was going back and see the same guy next day. ... Say, you don't suppose Samson went down there to get some lessons on how to pull a job?"

"I wouldn't know," I said. "Did he go back the next day?"

"I don't know," he said. "I had more important things to do than trail around after a do-gooder."

"Did Carter keep up his interest in crime prevention?"

"I don't know. Never heard him mention it again." He threw back his head and laughed with a barking sound. "Doesn't look like he did, seeing what happened this week, huh?"

"Who was the man in prison he went to see?" I asked.

"I don't know."

"You mean he didn't tell you?"

"He told me, all right, but I don't remember. I told you it was five years ago. Who the hell's going to remember some convict's name that long?"

This time it was me who signaled for another Canadian Club for him. I wanted him to work a little harder at remembering.

"You must remember something about it," I said. "Maybe what the guy was in for?"

He shrugged. "How do I know? It was something pretty big, I guess. I remember he was a guy who was on the front pages for a couple of days. I think he had some kind of a Spic name. Something like it, anyway. But I wasn't interested. I was just curious what Samson was up to."

"Okay," I said. I didn't think he had anything more to tell me, and I'd had about as much of him as I wanted. I stood up. "Thanks, Harder."

I don't think he heard me. He was staring off into the distance, shaking his head. "Think of it," he said. "A little jerk like that grabbing himself seven hundred thousand clams. ..."

I left him like that. I had an idea that Samson Carter was going to furnish George Harder most of his conversation for a long time. I was beginning to feel that I knew Samson Carter, and I thought he might be amused by that.

THREE

New York's Public Library on 42nd Street has always been one of the most interesting spots in the city to me. Here is a real cross-section of America. You can see all types there. Businessmen looking up whatever it is businessmen look for in books; students boning up for an exam; itinerant readers looking for the latest romance or mystery; little dried-up scholars who spend a lifetime delving into the erotic life of the Lamellibranchiata; furtive students of esoterica creeping through the contents of the locked shelves. A generous sprinkling of those the featherheads of press and politics now delight in calling eggheads.

I went into the newspaper room and started through the papers of five years earlier. Since I had to check only the front pages, it didn't take too long to cover the whole year. There were plenty of front-page crime stories, but when I was through I was sure I had the one I was looking for.

June 22, five years ago. A guy named Vasco Lopes had been arrested. A naturalized American, originally from Portugal. Two years earlier he had pulled a big robbery and then vanished. The interesting thing was that he had been trailed to Lisbon and had vanished from there. He was caught finally because he drank too much and talked too much to the wrong person. He had come right back to America, entering the country as a Brazilian national. He might have continued to get away with it if he'd have kept his mouth shut.

Downstairs I called the insurance company and got the name of Carter's bank. I had a hunch. Then I called the bank, identified myself, and told them what I wanted. They weren't happy about it but promised to look up the records. They told me to call them back in an hour.

I had something to eat and went on to the address where Carter had lived.

The rooming house looked like a million others. The cop was out front. I showed him the note, and he waved me on. I walked up five steps and rang the bell.

The landlady was a Mrs. Frasur. She was a little woman with white hair and birdlike eyes. Maybe sixty years old. Before she knew what I wanted, she had checked me with a rooming-house gaze. She probably knew how much my suit cost, and had guessed I would invite girls up to my room.

When I mentioned Carter's name, her face softened. I didn't have to be told that he had been one of her favorite roomers.

She led the way into a musty living room and sat down opposite me. "Poor Mr. Carter," she said. "I just won't believe he did all the terrible things the police say he did. I know something must have happened to him."

"What was he like?" I asked.

"He was a perfect gentleman," she said firmly. "He lived here for fifteen years and never gave me a day's trouble. He kept his room so neat, it hardly ever needed cleaning. He was so quiet you'd hardly know he was up there. And he always paid his rent the first of every month. A perfect gentleman."

"I'm sure he was," I said. "Did he have any friends, Mrs. Frasur?"

"Well, he was a very friendly man. But he didn't go out drinking and gambling and running around with a lot of roughnecks, if that's what you mean."

"What about girlfriends?"

She made a face. "He didn't have any use for the young chippies that are around these days. He was a decent man and he wouldn't have anything to do with them."

"If he didn't like girls," I said, "maybe he liked boys."

Her face tightened with anger. "He did not," she said indignantly. "Young man, I've been running a rooming house for thirty years, and I know all kinds the minute I lay eyes on them. Mr. Carter was a gentleman. Decent and respectable, he was."

"Uh-huh," I said.

"He was interested in other things," she said. "He read a lot of books. Was real cultured, if you know what I mean. And he was always studying. He went to night school one night every week. He was studying some foreign language. He used to tell me that he was going to retire when he was forty-two and go live in South America. I always told him he wouldn't be happy among all them foreigners."

I was sure that South America wouldn't mean a thing. If Carter had intended going there, he wouldn't have mentioned it. He had probably amused himself with half-truths. "He's just forty-two now, isn't he?" I asked. "And in a way, it could be said that he has retired."

"Mr. Carter would never have done the things they're

saying he did," she said grimly. "Nor any of the other horrible things you're hinting at. If he had been that kind of man, I wouldn't have had him in my house for fifteen years. I'll have you understand that I run a decent house and—"

"I'm sure you do," I said soothingly. "If you're certain he didn't do it, Mrs. Frasur, what do you think did happen?"

"I just know something terrible happened to him," she said. "He was such a nice gentleman. Studious and intellectual, if you know what I mean. Not like some that come into this house." Her expression included me in this latter vague group. She lived in a world where there were only nice people and people who weren't nice. And the nice people never did things like sleeping with other people or murdering them.

"Didn't he do anything else?" I asked. "Most people have hobbies. You know, stamp collecting, making ceramics, things like that."

"He did wonderful tricks," she said. "Just like a real magician, you know. Why, sometimes he used to put on a whole show just for me. And the kids. You just ask around the neighborhood. He used to spend hours out on the steps doing tricks for the children. All of them loved him." She said this triumphantly, as though the love of children proved he was incapable of being numbered among the people who weren't nice.

"I'm just beginning to find out about Mr. Carter," I told her, "but I'm sure that if I had known him I would have liked him as well as you do. Still, everything must be checked if we're to find out what did happen to him. I'd like to look at his room, if I may."

"Well, I guess you can," she said uncertainly. She couldn't make up her mind whether I was an enemy or a friend. She went over and took a key from the wall. "It's the first door on the right at the top of the stairs. But, mind you, don't go mussing things up. I've got better things to do than be cleaning up after a lot of dirty men."

"I will be very careful," I told her.

She surrendered the key reluctantly, and I went out into the hall. There was a pay phone there. I called the bank. They made me wait long enough to have to dig up another dime, but then I got my information.

On June 24, two days after the arrest of Vasco Lopes and one day after Carter had first visited him, Samson Carter had withdrawn a thousand dollars from his bank account. It was the only big withdrawal he had ever made until the day he closed the account.

I went upstairs and let myself into the room. It was neat. I was sure that the police hadn't left it that way; Mrs. Frasur must have put everything back in its proper place after they were through. I suspected it was pretty much as Carter had left it. After fifteen years she probably knew where everything belonged.

There were really two parts to the room. They could be separated at a glance. The furniture was all Mrs. Frasur's and in a way it looked like her. Prim and proper. Comfortable but not luxurious. It didn't interest me.

Samson Carter had left most of his private possessions behind. Some of his clothes were still in the dresser and the closet. Everything was neatly folded or hung up. There was no doubt they were Carter's clothes. They fit the picture that was building up in my mind.

The only pieces of furniture that were Carter's were a small phonograph-radio combination and a bookcase. There were a lot of records—classical music. I went over and picked through them. About a third of them were by Spanish composers. There were the concertos of Heitor Villa-Lobos. There were two comic operas—*La Bruja* by Ruperto Chapi and *La Verbena de la Paloma* by Tomás Bretón. There were several albums of folk music by Federico Chueca and one album of Édouard Lalo.

I turned to the other records. They fit in better with my picture of Carter. There was plenty of Bach. It looked to me like he had every concerto that Bach had written. There were albums of concertos by Frederick Delius, Ernest Bloch, and Béla Bartók. I straightened up and glanced at the phonograph. There was a record on the turntable. I switched it on and waited for it to warm up. Then I put the needle down.

I was listening to the throbbing quarter-note chords of the opening of the Second Violin Concerto by Bartók. I listened through that restless passage of the first idea, then abruptly shut it off before I could get caught up in the sweep of Bartók's Magyar rhythms. This was no time to start listening to music.

Next to the music albums there were several language records. All of them Spanish.

Carter had left a number of false clues around. The train ticket to Chicago, probably the reference to retiring in South America, maybe others that would still come to light. I wondered if the Spanish studies were part of that. I didn't think so. It wasn't as limiting as it might seem at first glance. It could mean that he'd planned on going somewhere that Spanish was spoken—or that he intended going elsewhere and pretending that Spanish was his native language.

I turned to the bookcase. Some of the books reflected the same taste the records had, but less restricted. Most of them were classics. *The Peloponnesian Wars* by Thucydides. The *Commentaries* of Caesar. *Chronicles of England, France, and Spain* by Jean Froissart. *The Autobiography of Benvenuto Cellini. The Prince* by Machiavelli. *The Conquest of Granada* by Washington Irving. *The Medici* by George F. Young. *A Discourse on Method* by René Descartes. *Gil Bias* by Alain René Lesage. *The Argentine Republic* by Ysabel F. Rennie. *The Forging of a Rebel* by Arturo Barea. There was only one volume of poetry: *El Gaucho Martín Fierro* by José Hernández. There wasn't much fiction. He had a complete collection of Henry James, *Shadows on the Pampas* by Ricardo Güiraldes, and *The Scandal* by Pedro Antonio de Alarcón.

The most prominent thing on the bookshelves was *Don Quixote.* There were four editions in English. The Motteux edition, first published in London in 1700; the John Ormsby edition; and the American editions of the Robinson Smith and the Samuel Putman translations. In Spanish, he had *El ingenioso hidalgo don Quijote de la Mancha* in seven volumes, and *El ingenioso hidalgo Don Quixote de la Mancha, compuesto por Miguel de Cervantes* in six volumes. All the editions showed handling.

There were several books on Spanish grammar and two Spanish-English dictionaries. They were all well worn.

Then I found the diaries. Twenty big fat volumes. One for each year. I stacked them on the floor and sat down. In every volume there were pages torn out. But in the other pages there was a complete record of the trivia that a man can perform in his lifetime. It helped to complete the picture of Carter, but that was all. It wasn't until I went back and started leafing through the first volume again that I found something interesting. Even then I almost missed it.

Twenty years before, Samson Carter had written a lot in his diary about his life having no purpose. It sounded like the sort of thing most people think when they're maybe sixteen, but not often as late as twenty-two. But within a couple of months all this had changed. It was there that for the first time there were pages torn out. And during the period when he was feeling sorry for himself, there were records showing that he had gone to see a Dr. Harrison Blake three times a week. There was just the mention of the appointments. After the torn pages there was no more reference to Dr. Blake.

I should have caught it the first time. Those steady appointments three times a week, on the part of someone who was emotionally disturbed, might mean a psychiatrist. And a psychiatrist might be able to shed more light on Carter—if he was still alive and if he still remembered a patient after twenty years.

There was a writing desk in one corner of the room. I went through it, knowing that if there'd been anything of value in it, the police would've already grabbed it. The only chance was that the cops and I might disagree on what was valuable.

It was filled with paid bills. Nothing else. Except for

a receipt from the Foster Magic Shop not far from Times Square. I stuck it in my pocket and shoved the other papers back.

I locked the door and went downstairs. I knocked on the door and she opened it so quickly she must have been standing right by it. I handed her the keys.

"You leave everything the way it was?" she asked.

"Exactly," I said. "Thanks for your help."

"You see his books?" she wanted to know. "A man who liked books that much wouldn't just walk off and leave them. That ought to prove to you that something terrible happened to him."

"Are you going to save the room for him?" I asked.

"He's paid up for the rest of the month," she said. "I wouldn't think of renting it before the end of the month."

"One more thing, Mrs. Frasur," I said. "When was the last time you saw Mr. Carter?"

"Wednesday morning when he left. He'd taken his suitcases down to Penn Station the day before. He was just starting his vacation, you know. To Chicago." She peered out at me. "Have they looked for him in Chicago?"

"They've looked," I said dryly. "Thanks again, Mrs. Frasur. If I ever need a rooming house, I'll be sure to look you up."

"I hardly ever have any vacancies," she said darkly.

I laughed and walked away. Down the street, I stopped in the drugstore and looked in the phone book. Dr. Harrison Blake was still listed. I called and told him that I'd like to see him about a former patient. He sounded pretty busy, but he finally agreed to see me the next morning.

The next stop was the magic shop. I just had enough time to make it and get into the offices of Great Northern.

There were a dozen men standing around inside the magic store. All of them were busily doing tricks for each other. One guy would do a trick and then everybody would try to top him. I leaned against the counter and waited until the owner finished showing some kid how to make a cigarette vanish. Then he came over to me.

I put the receipt on the counter. "Remember this guy?" I asked.

He looked at it. "Mr. Carter," he said. "Sure. … He's the same one who did that jewelry robbery this week, isn't he?"

I nodded. "Did you know him well?"

He shrugged. "He was a customer," he said. "He'd been coming in here for several years and buying a few things. We never talked about anything but magic."

"Was he good?" I asked.

"Pretty good. Like a lot of amateurs, he did two or three things well and that was it. Golf balls, a couple of thimble routines, and that was about all."

"When was he in last?"

"Maybe a month ago?"

"Remember what he bought?" I asked.

He glanced at the receipt. "This was it," he said. "A dozen golf balls and three shells—why three, I don't know. Some thimbles and two decks of cards."

"That was all?"

"That's it," he said. His manner indicated there was no point in talking about it any longer. I agreed with him. I picked up the receipt and put it back in my pocket. I sidestepped some guy who was doing an energetic back-palm and left.

It was a few minutes before five when I arrived at Great Northern. John Franklin was waiting for me. He looked like he'd been pacing up and down since he dropped me off that morning. His office was big enough for a lot of pacing. But it was also equipped for some fine sitting—with big, upholstered leather chairs—which interested me more at the time.

"Pretty good for a cop," I said, dropping into one of the chairs and waving at the room.

"Yeah," he said. "How'd you make out, Milo?"

"Pretty good," I said. "I talked to four people at length about Carter and I came up with four different pictures of him. Stone sees him as a lover of diamonds and that's all. The cops think he's just another scheming crook and cold-blooded killer. A guy who worked with him still thinks he's a jerk and wonders what the hell he's going to do with the loot. His landlady sees him as a studious book lover who wouldn't do anything nasty to girls and who was too tidy to do anything like a murder."

"I know," he said. "I'd noticed that everybody had a different idea of him. That means Carter doesn't go by anybody else's rules. And that's why I said it takes imagination to get anywhere on this case."

I nodded. "I'm getting a pretty good idea of my own about him," I said. "And you know something, Franklin—I'm beginning to like the little guy."

He looked worried for a minute. "Is that going to interfere with you taking him?"

I grinned at him. "You couldn't pry me off the case," I said. "I don't approve of murder even if it's committed by someone I like. And I'd rather take him myself than have some cop do it."

"You can be as gentle as you like," he said, "as long as we get that diamond back."

"As long as you're willing to pay the running expenses, I'll get it back," I said. "Now I want you to do something. Get on the phone and without tipping that it's related to this case, find a guy for me. Vasco Lopes. He was arrested five years ago on June 22. I want to know where he is now."

"What did you find?" he asked, reaching for the phone.

"Something the cops haven't yet," I said. I saw his look. "Sure, I'm being evasive. I don't like to talk about my ideas. That way there's no leak and no one telling me how they think I ought to handle it. That's the way I work. Take it or leave it." I said it gently so he wouldn't get angry.

"We'll take it," he said. "Results are all that mean anything, and you've always delivered those." He got busy on the phone. He talked to somebody on the force and then hung up.

"Vasco Lopes," he said, turning back to me, "is in Sing Sing. Doing ten to twenty."

"Good," I said. "Now I want something else. Arrange for me to see him. Tonight."

He whistled softly. "That's a bigger order," he said. "You've got to get a smallpox shot. By the time you can reach the prison, it'll be late. Why not do it early in the morning before your plane?"

"I've got another appointment in the morning. It has to be tonight."

"It'll be way past visiting hours. The warden won't like it."

I made a suggestion about the warden. "What's the matter? Isn't this company important enough to swing a little influence with seven hundred thousand bucks at stake?"

"I think so," he said gravely. "Wait a minute." He left the office.

When he came back there was another man with him. An older man with just enough gray in his hair to set off the Florida tan. He was the kind who looked more at home at a director's meeting than anywhere else, unless it was the country club.

"This is Milo March," John Franklin said. "Milo, this is Mr. Delaney. Mr. Delaney is the executive vice-president of Great Northern."

He gave me a limp hand to shake. It's a funny thing about vice-presidents. You take a guy when he's working his way up; he'll have one of those locker-room handshakes and his ideas will veer according to the wind. Then he finally makes the grade. Right away his mind becomes rigid and his hand goes limp.

"How are you, March?" he said with what he thought was a friendly tone. He was going to prove he was democratic if it killed him. "John here tells me you've done some fine work for us. Glad to see you're working with us again."

What can you say to a guy like that? I settled for a low-pitched "Ummm."

"Now," he said briskly, having finished consorting with the help, "what's this about wanting to see a prisoner in Sing Sing tonight?"

"That's it," I said.

"What is the purpose?" he asked.

"I think he may help me find where Samson Carter has gone."

"How?"

Before I could answer that one, John Franklin jumped in ahead of me. "March rather likes to work pretty much on his own, sir. Since his methods have been so successful in the past, I'm letting him play this the way he sees fit."

"I see," Mr. Delaney said. He saw, all right, and he didn't like it. He was a man who expected answers when he asked questions. But he decided to let it pass. "It could be arranged, of course. The warden is a very good friend of mine and so is the governor. But it's quite irregular. I'm not sure we should do it."

"Okay," I said cheerfully. "It's your seven hundred thousand dollars."

That got him. I was talking about a number he loved. "I will get in touch with the warden and see what can be done," he said.

He marched stiffly out of the office. John Franklin and I grinned at each other.

"He'll get over it," I said. "He'll run over to his club later and have a spot of Irish whiskey and branch water and forget all about it. It'll do him good to have the help talk back once in a while."

He was still a little nervous about it. "I hope you're right," he said. "We might as well get the other thing out of the way while we're waiting."

He took me down to another office. One of the insurance company's doctors was there. He examined me and then gave me a smallpox shot. That's all there was to it.

"That'll get you in almost anywhere," Franklin said as we walked back to his office.

When we got there, the vice-president's secretary was waiting for us. She said that the warden would be expecting Mr. March. I watched the movement of her hips as she walked out. It was a high-level wiggle, as though every inch of her knew how important her boss was. I grinned to myself, but didn't say anything to Franklin. He probably wouldn't have understood; if he could have, he wouldn't be in the job he was. That's the trouble with seeing too much. It keeps your head bumping against those upper rungs.

"Want me to go up with you?" Franklin said.

"If you'd like the ride. I don't want you going in with me, but I wouldn't mind having someone drive me up."

"I'll do it. Anything else?"

"Yeah," I said. "A thousand dollars."

He looked his question.

"Better charge it up to general expenses," I said. "Mr. Delaney wouldn't approve of what I'm going to do with it."

He nodded and left. When he came back, he handed me a stack of bills. "I thought you'd rather have it in small bills," he said.

"Good," I said. I counted the money. There was a thousand dollars. I tucked it away in my pocket.

"I thought somebody might make a mistake and slip in a couple of extra bills," I explained. "But I guess I'll have to work for my money."

He laughed, but it didn't sound natural. People who work in banks or insurance companies are never amused about mistakes with money.

We went downstairs to a restaurant and had dinner. Then we got in Franklin's car and headed north. I leaned back against the seat and went to sleep before he could start a conversation.

FOUR

Night fog out of the river had turned Sing Sing into a gray ghost castle. Our headlights picked at it through the fog and I felt myself shiver. But only partly from the cold. The fog made the outside look even more like it was on the inside where everything was gray—including the hopes of most of the men there.

They kept us at the gate until a captain of guards came down. John Franklin stayed with the guards, but the Captain took me back and into the main prison. He was a surly man, the expression on his face being, I imagine, little different from that of the other inmates. He didn't say anything until he had shown me into a small room.

"Wait here," he said. He closed the door and left.

There was nothing in the room but a metal table and two plain chairs. The walls were whitewashed and antiseptic-looking. I sat in one of the chairs and lighted a cigarette.

After a bit the door opened and a man stepped inside. Beyond him a guard stood at the door. I had specified that I had to see the prisoner alone, so I stared at the guard and waited. He finally closed the door. I shifted my gaze to the prisoner.

He wore faded gray denim. A black number was stenciled across it. He was tall and well built, probably about my own age. He had black hair and dark skin. Women would have considered him handsome. His face was locked in a kind of hardness that left no room for emotion. Only his eyes were alive, and they watched me with a steady wariness. The guards wouldn't have told him anything about me, but late visits were not part of the regulations. Prisoners know that the unusual is not to be trusted. They learn the hard way.

I pushed my cigarettes over in front of the other chair.

"Cigarette?" I said.

"Sure," he said. He stepped over and took a cigarette but remained standing. I tossed him my matches. He caught them and lit the cigarette without taking his gaze from me. He put the matches down on the table.

"You're Vasco Lopes?" I said.

"Yeah."

I sat and smoked without saying any more. He scuffed his feet on the concrete floor.

"Who're you?" he asked finally.

"Milo March," I said. I knew it wouldn't mean anything to him.

"Copper?" he asked.

I shook my head. "Not exactly," I said. "I'm an insurance detective. You might call me a cop, but a cop wouldn't."

Something flickered through his eyes. It might have been the beginning of a smile. If it was, it never reached his lips. "Insurance?" he said. He was in for armed robbery. He couldn't see any connection. "What's that got to do with me?"

"Maybe nothing," I said. "Maybe a lot. Why don't you sit down?"

He was curious by this time. It took some of the edge off the hostility he felt for anyone who could walk in or out of this place as he wanted to. He pulled back the chair and sat down.

"I want to know something," I said.

His face tightened again. "I ain't no squealer," he said. For the first time I noticed the barest trace of an accent in his voice.

"I know you're not," I told him. "I'm not exactly asking you to blow the whistle on anyone. What I'm asking you will never be repeated to the cops."

This time he outwaited me.

"Five years ago," I said, "the day after you were arrested, a little guy went to see you in the Tombs. You probably don't remember his name, even if he told you, but it was Samson Carter."

He'd forgotten but he remembered quickly. He looked interested.

"The next day," I said, "the little guy came back. This time he gave you a thousand dollars. In cash."

That surprised him. I could see that he thought no one knew about that. And it made him more curious.

"I want to know what you told him for that thousand dollars," I said. I waited a minute. "When you tell me, I'll give you another thousand dollars. In cash."

He tried to read the answers in my face. But I wasn't giving anything away either. "Maybe," he said, "he wanted me to tell him how to pull a job." He was fishing.

I shook my head. "I think I know why he came to see you and was willing to pay a thousand dollars," I said. "Want to hear my guess?"

"Go ahead," he said. "It's your visit. I ain't going anyplace."

"You were an American citizen," I said. "You pulled a big job and then you went to Lisbon and vanished. The cops probably notified the police of every country and then sat back, hoping somebody would fish you up for them. But in the meantime you came straight back to America. Only you came in on a Brazilian passport and with an American visa. They were all in order and nobody thought of questioning them. You stayed away from the places where anyone had known you. If you'd kept your mouth shut, you might never have been caught. The cops were looking for an American citizen they thought was out of the country, not a Brazilian citizen sitting in their laps."

Something flickered through his eyes again. I decided that was as far as he ever went with laughing.

"That's not guessing," he said. "All of that was in the papers."

"Sure," I said. "I think the little guy paid you a thousand dollars to tell him the name of the man in Lisbon who provided you with the Brazilian passport."

His face closed up so completely I knew I was right.

"All I want," I said, "is to talk to the man in Lisbon. Then I'll forget I ever heard his name. And I'm willing to pay a thousand dollars." I took out the stack of money and put it on the table halfway between us.

It took him a long time to make up his mind. Finally he reached out and pulled the money over to his side. He glanced through it, doing a rough count.

"All I told him," he said, "was Manuel Maria Tristão. Rua

Fragoso, in the Arab Alfama quarter. Number twenty-one."
The stack of money vanished.

I nodded and stood up.

"The little guy," he said. "Why'd he want it? He looked like an honest John."

"He was an honest John," I said. "Only last Wednesday he killed a guard and knocked off a diamond worth seven hundred thousand dollars. Except for that one little thing, he's still an honest John."

His mouth was still open as I walked out and nodded to the guard.

John Franklin didn't say anything until we were well away from the prison.

"Well?" he said finally.

I grinned in the darkness. "I spent your thousand bucks," I said. "But I know where to go when I get to Lisbon."

"Where Carter is?"

"No. But it's the jumping-off place for Carter." I laughed to myself. "You know something? The more I hear about this little guy, the better I like him. He did something that no professional would ever think of doing and got himself the answer he wanted. As simple as that, where every crook would have had to make it complicated. You know Gregory's theory that every crook in the world will be after Carter and the diamond?"

"I know about it."

"I'll bet they never get within shouting distance," I said. "Carter doesn't know any of the rules. He's playing everything strictly by ear and it's going to confuse the hell out of cops and crooks alike."

"I know," Franklin said. When he spoke again his tone was dry. "My only consolation is that we've got a man on his trail who also doesn't pay any attention to rules."

I let it ride and went back to sleep. Franklin woke me up when we reached the hotel where he'd made a reservation for me. I went upstairs and resumed my sleeping where it had broken off.

I was up early the next morning. I had breakfast in the hotel and then went to Great Northern.

There was a last-minute pep talk from another Great Northern vice-president while Franklin watched me with a nervous eye. Then Franklin handed me two thousand dollars for expenses and assured me there'd be more if it was needed. He tried to hint that they'd all take it kindly if I kept in touch by phone. Reversed charges, of course. I was generous about it. I promised to send him a postcard.

Taking my luggage with me, I got a cab and gave the driver the address of Dr. Harrison Blake. I would go directly from his office to the airport.

The doctor's office was in the eighties just off Central Park West. He didn't keep me waiting long. He was a brisk little man of about sixty. He got even more brisk when he discovered that I was the man who had called him the night before. He looked over my identification as if he expected to find a collapsed synapse.

"What can I do for you, Mr. March?" he asked.

"I was stabbing in the dark when I called you last night," I said. "Maybe I'd better know what kind of doctor you are before I waste your time more."

"I'm a psychoanalyst," he said. He smiled briefly. "You need my services, Mr. March?"

"Probably," I said, "but that's not why I'm here. Twenty years ago, for a period of about two months, you had a patient by the name of Samson Hercules Carter. Do you suppose you still have any records on him?"

"Samson Hercules Carter?" he said. "Didn't I see that name in the papers recently? In connection with a murder?"

"That's the one," I said.

He looked interested. "I thought there was something familiar about the name," he said. "Wait a minute, Mr. March."

He got up and went into the next room. He was gone ten or fifteen minutes. When he came back, he was carrying a book.

"You're in luck," he said. "I wouldn't normally keep records on a case which was terminated after such a short period, but there were a number of things about Mr. Carter that interested me. I was working on a book at the time—it was published five years later—and I included him in the book. Before we go farther, however, I think I should know a little more about the circumstances."

I quickly told him the story of what had happened on Wednesday, leaving out the things I'd learned since. His interest took a big leap when I told him about the diamond.

"Excellent," he said. He looked at me eagerly. "Do you suppose I might be permitted to examine him when he's captured?"

"I imagine it might be arranged," I said. "Depending on your opinion, you might even be welcomed by the defense." I hesitated and then put something I'd been thinking into words. "I have never met Carter, but my own personal opinion is that he lives in a world entirely of his own making. In a strict moral sense I don't think he is a criminal. Of course, he can't be allowed to get away with this, but he certainly shouldn't be executed. If you can do anything about that, then I think the defense should certainly retain you."

"No one should be executed," the doctor said. "It serves no purpose except to satisfy a revenge motive which is out of our barbaric past. ... The story of Samson Carter is in this book and I will give you a copy. But if you like I will briefly outline it for you."

"I'd like it very much," I said.

He nodded. "Do you know anything about psychoanalysis, Mr. March?"

"Not much."

"There are many theories in the field," he said. "I, and a number of my colleagues, have long believed that much neurosis is a sort of emptiness in the individual—you will notice that my book is called *The Empty Ones.* You might speak of it as structure without content. The individual is unable to find any permanent values within himself and is constantly looking outside for the fulfillment lacking within him. He feels himself to be an alien in the world. Consequently he is constantly confused between reality and fantasy and is always in danger of accepting his fantasies as the only reality. This is, of course, an oversimplification, but perhaps it gives you an idea."

I nodded.

"Carter was such a person," he said. "He came to me

because he felt that he was empty, that there was no purpose to his life. He abruptly terminated the visits because he believed he had suddenly discovered a goal and that this was no longer true. He did not tell me what this goal was, but at the time I suspected that it was another fantasy. From what you've told me, I'd guess that he finally moved into that world of fantasy."

"Perhaps," I said. I didn't want to tell him any more until I'd heard what he had to say.

"In the short time we had," he went on, "I was unable to get the complete history of Carter. But I did learn that his father was a big, boisterous man. The father was delighted when he had a son and was immediately convinced that his son would be the biggest and best of men when he grew up. He expressed this by naming the infant Samson Hercules. When the son turned out to be small and delicate, more interested in books than barbells, the father took it as a personal betrayal. He never forgave his son. It was the father who started laughing over the fact that this puny male was named Samson Hercules. It was a laughter which was to continue through school and into adult life."

The story of Samson Carter, I was thinking, could rightfully be called a horror story. I'd felt that from the beginning. "Could you say," I asked, "that this made him feel that he had to do something important, something that would make him a big man, yet also convinced him that he could never do it?"

"Something like that. He was convinced that he could never do anything important in the world of reality. But in the world of fantasy he could do anything. There, you see, he could be a big man. As big as his father. It was probably some such fantasy that made him stop the visits here."

I nodded. It was immediately after the last visit to the doctor that the first pages were torn from Carter's diary. And from the little I had picked up, I'd guess that it was immediately after this that Carter started the preparations that had culminated last Wednesday.

"I think so," I told the doctor. "It was shortly after that when Carter started putting half of his savings in diamonds. This was obviously not done just as an investment. We also believe that Carter started planning twenty years ago. Not that he intended stealing the specific diamond he did—its existence was not even known then. But I think he started with the idea of saving enough money and eventually stealing a large diamond. Not for gain, but to possess."

"The diamonds are interesting," Dr. Blake said. "When Samson Carter was a small boy, his father owned something which is rarely seen these days. It was a piece of crystal, glass, with a picture of himself inside it. It was a cheap souvenir of something or other, but the boy played with it for hours at a time. For a while he was convinced that the picture imbedded in the glass was his father. In fact, I got the impression that the father in the glass was more real to him than the father who walked about the house."

"The one in the glass was probably kinder to him," I said.

He nodded. "When his father died, shortly before he first came to me, he tried to find the picture in the crystal, but it had apparently been lost. Perhaps the diamond is merely a substitute for the lost glass."

I thought a minute. "Tell me what you think of this, Doctor," I said. "I think that Carter's plan was this: He would save enough money to last him the rest of his life. Then he would take the diamond—he had decided on the Tavernier Blue when he first saw it five years ago and had eventually convinced himself that it rightfully belonged to him—and go away. He had prepared himself for twenty years so that he could live almost as a native in the place he had chosen. After twenty years he saw the whole thing so clearly that it was a reality to him long before he put it into operation. During this period, while he is making it come true, he is dangerous. He will kill anyone who interferes, not cold-bloodedly in the terms the police use, but merely because the person intrudes. But once he has arrived at his destination, he will settle into a new personality and probably never commit so much as a misdemeanor again."

"Unless someone again intrudes on the reality he has constructed," the doctor said. "Of course, you understand, this is a sketchy analysis because we do not have all the facts. It may be wrong in a dozen places."

"It feels right," I said.

There was no more the doctor could tell me. I thanked him and left, taking the book with me. I would read it on the plane, but I was sure I had most of it already.

It was well after noon when I reached LaGuardia. I had lunch in the restaurant and then waited in the terminal. When the flight to Lisbon was announced, I went out and climbed into the plane.

The Pan American Clipper scraped over the roofs of Long

Island apartment houses and gained altitude. Below, New York was once more a sprawling old woman, shrinking rapidly as we headed out over the Atlantic.

He'd arrived in Lisbon on Thursday. He had checked into the hotel. Taking the few things that were important, he had walked out of the hotel and no one had seen him go. He had asked for directions in Spanish and within a few minutes he stood in front of Number 21. It was an old art shop, its window black with dirt. A bell jangled as he opened the door.

For a price Senhor Tristão was happy to give him what he wanted. It would be ready not later than Monday. Certainly no later than Tuesday.

This was not soon enough. He knew that on Sunday another plane would leave New York and be in Lisbon on Monday. He insisted on having it at once.

Senhor Tristão protested that it was a work of art and that as an artist he could not be rushed. Such matters took time.

They finally compromised. It would be ready by Saturday night.

It was Senhor Tristão who found him a room in the neighborhood and who sent him to Carlos Sarmento, whose knife was always for hire. The arrangements were quickly made.

Friday and Saturday were spent in shopping. New luggage, new clothes. Everything must be new. Almost everything. Then there was his new mustache, a thin, dark line across his upper lip. Three days were not enough, but it showed prom-

ise. It had elegance. That was the important thing. It had not been grown as a disguise but because it now belonged. He was also an artist in his way.

Saturday evening he again went to the art shop in the Rua Fragoso. In the back room, beyond the paintings which no one had wanted to buy in years, he sat stiffly while Senhor Tristão took his photograph. A print was quickly made. He did not like it. It was too light. The next one was too dark. He nodded when he saw the third print. It was soon dry and was glued into place.

Payment was made. In small diamonds as had been agreed. Senhor Tristão examined each one, clucking over it as he discovered it to be genuine. As he approved of each one, he tucked it away in the pocket of a greasy vest. When the last of the diamonds had been examined, adding up to more than twice his usual price, he handed over the passport he had made with his usual care. Then he, in turn, waited for approval.

It came in an unexpected fashion.

He knew that the passport must be good, so he did not even look at it. He put it in his pocket and when his hand came out it held the gun. A look of surprise came over the face of Senhor Tristão. It was still there a moment later when he fell to the floor and died with the taste of his own blood in his mouth.

He felt neither triumph nor regret at the death of Senhor Tristão. It had been a necessity. If the trail were to end in Lisbon, there could be no markers left to point in the new direction. He put the two unused photographs in his pocket.

He was an honest man and he did not take back the diamonds which now belonged to the corpse. He left the shop.

There were always loud noises—and many of them sounded like gunshots—in the Alfama quarter of Lisbon and no one paid any attention to the latest one. Nor saw him leave the shop.

On Sunday a small passenger plane lifted from the Lisbon airport. The sun made golden streaks through the windows. He sat in one of the wing seats and breathed the air of a new world. Cupping his hands around it so that others might not see, he looked into the blue diamond. It caught a bit of the sunlight and held it prisoner deep within the blueness. He stared at this sign of life until his cupped hand ached. Then he put the diamond away.

FIVE

From the air, Lisbon has always reminded me of a picture postcard. The water is bluer than water should be. The sun shining on the buildings make them seem whiter than they are. The whole thing seems more like a four-color process job than reality. Then, as the plane drops lower, the air of illusion goes and you see Lisbon as she is—which is still one of the prettiest and cleanest cities in Europe.

The red tape at the airport didn't take long and I was soon through with it. I took a taxi and went first to the police station.

I was expected and the way was more or less cleared for me. The insurance company and the New York cops had both been in touch with them and asked them to cooperate. They assured me that they hadn't rested since first receiving word that Senhor Carter was in Lisbon. They were polite about it, but the implication was that if they couldn't find him, I was wasting my time. They were convinced that the Senhor Carter knew he didn't have a chance against the Polícia International e de Defesa do Estado and had chosen suicide as the only graceful way out. He had probably taken a boat out and then leaped overboard. As for the rest, it was undoubtedly in the hands of God and the sharks.

"More likely in the belly of the shark," I said.

This convulsed them. They spent the next thirty minutes telling me what a funny fellow I was. When it was finally established that we were all good fellows together, we got around to the reason I had stopped there in the first place. I wanted to take a look at Carter's hotel room and I wanted to do it without benefit of a parade.

By this time they were very understanding. They could understand that a representative of the insurance company might want to look at the room of the suicide—it had jumped from theory to fact—and they weren't insulted by the fact that I wanted to go alone.

We exchanged a number of compliments about Portugal and the United States, and I finally got away. They had arranged with the hotel to have me admitted to Carter's room. It had only taken an hour to transact five minutes' business.

First I went to the Avenida Palace Hotel and checked in. The Aviz was too rich for my blood, even on an expense account. It was still early in the day and I was sure that Carter was no longer in Lisbon. I decided to rest before I tried his room. The shot I'd had Saturday night was working on me and I felt feverish.

Later I went downstairs and had a couple of brandies. It put enough strength in my legs so that I felt like going on. I took a taxi over to the Aviz.

It is one of the most expensive hotels in Lisbon. The lobby was filled with people, at least half of them Americans. It was almost the cocktail hour and the Lisbon night life was starting to show some movement. I went over to the desk.

"My name is Milo March," I said. I was speaking Spanish,

but nearly everyone in Portugal understands it. "I believe that it has been arranged for me to see one of your rooms."

The desk clerk looked as if he thought I might walk off with the hotel silverware. "Yes, Mr. March," he said. The fact that he answered me in English was another sign of his disapproval. "You understand, Mr. March, that we have left Mr. Carter's things in the room only because he insisted on paying a week in advance. The manager, however, has asked me to tell you that we shall remove the things tonight. If Mr. Carter returns later, we will give him a refund. But the Aviz Hotel is not accustomed to—"

"Don't strain yourself, Buster," I said. "Just give me the key and tell me which room. After that I don't care what you do with Carter's things. But if you're hard-pressed, I can make a suggestion."

He knew English well enough to get my meaning. His face paled and his mouth set like an old maid's on being shown a red-light district. He reached around behind him and got a key. He handed it to me gingerly.

"Room four fifty-three," he said with distaste. "Don't dirty the room up."

I grinned at him. "Relax, bud," I said. *"Todo saldrá en la colada."*

I turned away before he could think of an answer. I walked across and entered the elevator. It was crowded, too. But I didn't mind too much. One of the people pressing up against me was a good-looking girl.

"Quatro," I told the operator.

The elevator shot upward and came to a jerky stop more or

less on the fourth floor. I reluctantly stepped away from the girl behind me. At the same time another man started out. We collided.

"Dispénseme," I said.

"Não, Senhor," he returned just as politely. *"Perdoe-me!"*

I took my first look at him. He was the Lisbon version of a Broadway sharpie. He was a little short guy, with a dark, mean-looking face. His suit was expensive, but it had too much padding in the shoulders. The color was just a shade too light. And the toes of his suede shoes were just a little too pointed. But if his clothes didn't fit the Aviz Hotel, his manners certainly did.

I waited for him to go ahead and he waited for me to go ahead. The rest of the people waited for both of us.

"Se faz favor, Senhor," he said, with a stiff little bow.

To hell with it, I thought. I wasn't going to stand around all day in an elevator trying to be more polite than he was. I nodded. *"Muchas gracias,"* I said, and stepped out. I thought I heard a collective sigh of relief behind me.

I glanced at the doors opposite the elevator. The number I wanted seemed to be to the right. I turned and walked down the corridor. Four fifty-three was near the end of the wing.

I put the key in the door and turned it. My hand was on the knob when I became aware that someone was directly behind me. Before I could turn, something pressed against my back between the shoulder blades. I didn't have to see it to know what it was. The point had already gone through my clothes and was tickling my skin. It was a knife. My guess was that an expert held it.

"Tome cuidado," he said softly. "Go in gently."

I went in gently. I turned the knob as carefully as if it had been wired. I swung the door inward and stepped very carefully inside the room. The point of a knife against your back commands respect in any language.

I heard the door close behind me. One of his hands felt quickly to see if I had a gun. I didn't. I'd left it back in Denver. It wouldn't have made much difference if I hadn't.

He grunted with satisfaction when he found none. "You may turn around, Senhor," he said. "It should not be said that Carlos Sarmento kills a man whose back is turned. But slowly, Senhor."

I turned around. Slowly. It was the man from the elevator. The one who had been so polite. He was holding the knife so that the point was less than an inch from my stomach. He held it like a professional.

"Qué desea usted?" I asked. *"Soy de los Estados Unidos—"*

"I know," he said. He smiled happily at me. "That is why I shall kill you. The Senhor Carter said that one would come today from the United States. The Senhor Carter is very smart."

I had to admit he was right. At first I'd thought that maybe I'd run into an overly enthusiastic display of ordinary anti-Americanism. Instead I'd been guilty of underestimating Carter. I was annoyed at myself.

"A favor?" I asked him. "A last cigarette?"

He frowned. Obviously he didn't want to waste any time, yet even in killing me he felt the need to be polite. It was a reasonable request. He nodded. "But move carefully, Senhor."

"Most carefully," I agreed. I took out a cigarette and matches, moving in slow motion. I could feel the muscles in my stomach tightening up like a drawn string, but my hand was steady as I lighted the cigarette. I dropped the match to the floor—and flipped the cigarette straight into his eyes. I threw myself sideways, chopping down with my right hand.

Even so, I was almost too slow. His arm had thrust forward purely by reflex. The blade sliced through my shirt and I felt a stinging along my right ribs. Then my fingers closed around his wrist.

He was strong, but I kept him slightly off balance so he couldn't use his entire strength. He almost had enough anyway. Twice he succeeded in turning the point of the knife in my direction and forcing it toward its goal. Twice I turned his wrist back in time. The third time I was ready for him. I shifted my position fast and used his lunge to twist his arm around. He said something between clenched teeth and dropped the knife.

I let go of his arm. He bent to reach for the knife. I was ready for that, too. I swung a low uppercut that caught him full on the nose and threw him back several feet. It must have hurt him, but he never let on. He merely dived for the knife again. Once more I hit him in the same spot. He was off balance and it sent him rolling across the floor. This time I struck oil. Red oil. The blood spurted out of his nose like a gusher.

He paid no attention to it. He scrambled to his feet and went for the knife once more. This time I stepped in to meet him and drove my right into the same target. I could feel the cartilage give away beneath my knuckles as his head snapped back. This time his breath came out in something that was just short of a scream.

He got to his feet slowly and stood there. The blood dripped down over his mouth and chin. His black eyes stared at me without blinking. I noticed the fingers of his right hand flexing as if they were closing about the handle of a knife.

I leaned down and picked up the knife. The blade was a good seven inches long and had been honed until it was as sharp as a razor. I tossed it on the bed behind me. Then I stepped on the cigarette, which was smoldering on the carpet.

"Now, Senhor Carlos Sarmento," I said, "let's have a little talk."

He said nothing. He just stood there, staring at me with those black, expressionless eyes.

I hated to do it, but I had no more time to waste on him. I wanted his side of the story and I wanted it fast.

I stepped in and swung as hard as I could. Once more on the exact center of his smashed nose. As he went down, he screamed. Not loudly, but it was still a scream. There are not many men who can stand much punishment on an already broken nose.

Before he could move, I reached down and jerked him to his feet. I hit him on the nose again and held him up. The breath rattled in his throat.

"*Bastante!*" he said hoarsely. "No more, Senhor."

I let him go. He wavered but managed to stay on his feet. Tears were rolling down his face and mixing with the blood.

I had to remind myself of the knife on the bed to keep from feeling sorry for him.

"Carter hired you?" I asked.

"Yes—Senhor." His gaze was fixed on the floor. One hand was cupped over his nose, muffling his words. He was breathing too fast and I had to strain to hear him.

"When and where?" I asked.

"Friday last. My house."

"How did he know about you?"

The pain was a raw sound in his voice. "My friend— Manuel Maria Tristão sent him to me."

"What happened when he came to see you?" I asked.

He hesitated. I reached out and tucked my fingers under the lapel of his coat. I could feel him shrinking away from my hand.

"No, Senhor," he said quickly. "I will talk." For just a moment his gaze came up to meet mine and something stirred deep within his eyes. It was strong enough to push the pain aside. I knew he was thinking how I'd look with a knife in my back.

"The Senhor Carter," he said, "told me he had a room here. The Aviz Hotel. But he was not staying in it. I was to come here and watch. He said the police would come—but they would leave everything alone. It was as he said. The Senhor Carter is a smart man."

"Very," I agreed dryly. "Go on."

"He said that sometime on Monday—today—a man from the United States would come. If he came alone—I was to kill him at once. If he came with others, I was to follow until he was alone. ... Now I have failed. My prayers to San Isidro were for nothing."

"You mean Carter knew I was coming?" I asked. "He described me?" I didn't see how anyone could have tipped him off—especially since I wasn't even on the case when he'd hired Carlos.

He shook his head and some of his blood splattered on his sleeve. "He did not know who it would be," he said. "But he was certain there would be a *norte-americano* looking for him."

Carter was smart, all right. I wondered if he'd been smart enough not to pay Carlos in advance. "What were you to get for this?" I asked.

"Senhor Carter gave me a diamond," he said. "It was small, but worth twenty-eight hundred escudos. He promised me ten more exactly like it."

"How were you going to collect them?" I asked.

His pain must have been less, for he smiled scornfully at the suggestion that he might have trusted a stranger. "Manuel Maria holds them. The Senhor Carter gave them to him in my presence. I am, after all, Senhor, a businessman."

I had been to Lisbon before and knew something of its inhabitants who were like Carlos and Manuel. I had a picture of Samson Carter among them, displaying his diamonds, and it seemed obvious that once again I must have underestimated him.

"If you saw him with all those diamonds," I said, "how is it that you didn't take steps to relieve him of them?"

"I thought of it," Carlos admitted. "Senhor Carter showed me his little diamonds when he first came to my room. He mentioned that I might be tempted by them. He pulled a gun from his pocket and put a bullet in my bed not two inches from my thigh. Then he put the gun away, smiling all the time. He said the bullet in my bed was to remind me that he would kill me if I tried to get his diamonds. I decided that perhaps Senhor Carter was more formidable than he looked." He paused and shrugged. "He was paying me well and there was no point in taking unreasonable chances."

I smiled to myself, remembering the four pictures of Samson Carter I'd gotten in New York. I wondered what they would have thought of Carlos's picture of Carter.

"He couldn't have been sure that someone would come today," I said. "What if no one had turned up?"

"Then I was to come back on Thursday when the next plane arrives from the United States."

"Where is Carter now?" I asked.

"I do not know, Senhor," he said. He sounded as if he were telling the truth.

"When was the last time you saw Carter or your friend?"

"Early on Friday, Senhor. Since then I have been here at the hotel each day until late at night. When I heard you at the desk, I thought that my vigil was finished."

I thought about it for a minute. I was sure that Carlos had told me all that he knew.

Before he knew what I was doing, I stepped forward and drove my fist into his jaw. He collapsed to the floor, unconscious. I picked him up and tossed him on the bed. Then I turned my attention to the room.

Carter's two suitcases were there. Both were filled with clothes and small possessions. The latter included his razor, hairbrush, toothbrush, and paste. Once they had probably been neatly packed, but that was before the Portuguese police had gone through them. But that's all there was of him in the room. I went through the clothes, but there was nothing in any of the pockets. They might have been a fine clue for backtracking Carter, but they were useless in showing where he'd gone.

He'd probably walked out with the clothes on his back, his diamonds and money, and his magic equipment. The new personality was going to be complete.

I went out and locked the door. Downstairs, I tossed the key on the desk in front of the clerk. *"Obrigado,"* I said. It was one of the few words in Portuguese I knew.

He picked up the key without saying anything. I could see he wanted to know if I'd found anything, but he couldn't bring himself to ask.

"I guess I did get the room a little dirty," I said, "but it was unavoidable."

"Oh?" he said coldly.

"Yeah," I said. I grinned at him. "I'm afraid I got blood all over the floor and the bed cover." I left while he was still trying to persuade himself that he'd heard wrong.

Out on the street, I decided to walk. There was no rush. The Alfama quarter would just be starting to come to life. If I walked, I could stop and get a brandy, which would do more for the way I felt than a ride in a taxi.

I stopped in the Rua Àurea and changed a few dollars into escudos. I went on to the Rossio where the streets are lined with cafés. The English had long ago named the Rossio "Rolling Motion Square" because of the black and white tile with which the sidewalk is paved. You can almost get a cheap drunk on by walking along the Rossio and keeping your gaze on the sidewalk.

I picked one of the cafés at random and sat down. I had strong Portuguese coffee heavily laced with brandy and began to feel better. I was getting low on cigarettes and had forgotten to bring more with me from the hotel. They had my favorite brand for thirty cents, which wasn't too much worse than in the States.

An hour later I was on my way again. It was almost ten years since the last time I was in Lisbon, but my sketchy memory of the city began coming back as I walked through the old streets. I remembered one thing that had always amused me. In Lisbon each street carries signs indicating the cross-street that's ahead of you, but there is practically never a sign giving the name of the street you're on. As a result you can always tell where you're going, but you never know where you are.

It was easy to tell when I started nearing the Alfama quarter. The pungent smell of the Tagus River began a personal assault on my nose. It was my hint to begin looking for the Rua Fragoso. After three or four false starts I found it—a winding, narrow street with dark alleys that defied the streetlights.

Like many of the others, Number 21 was a shop in front, probably with living quarters in the rear. The sign announced that it was an art shop, and the single flyspecked oil painting in the window bore feeble witness to the fact. The combination of grime on the window and the flyspecks on the picture made it almost impossible to tell what the painting was. It seemed to be a crude replica of the Castelo do São Jorge, which still looms over the city, reminding Lisbon of a history going back to the twelfth century. It had probably, I guessed, been painted by the occupant of Number 21 before he discovered that there were more profitable aspects to art.

I went down the four steps to the door. It was locked. I knocked lightly and waited. There was no answer. I knocked again. A little louder. There was no light visible in the store, but that didn't mean there was no one there. I pounded still harder on the door.

I must have been standing there, pounding occasionally on the door, for five minutes before I became aware that someone was standing above me on the sidewalk. I turned to look at him.

He was an old man in ragged clothes and with a wool cap on his head. It was hard to tell his age, as it often is in Portugal. He might have been sixty or he might have been in his seventies. His dark face was lined, but his eyes were young and sharp. He reminded me of an amiable pirate. Which was probably what he was.

"The Senhor is looking for someone?" he asked. Or, at least, that's what I thought he asked. The Portuguese never have any trouble understanding Spanish, but knowing Spanish will only help a little when someone is speaking Portuguese. I had never learned to speak the language, although at one time I could understand it fairly well.

"For the Senhor Tristão," I said. "It is important that I see him soon. Is it known where he can be found?"

"There is perhaps disagreement as to where he is at the moment," he said. "The Senhor comes from afar?"

"From the United States," I admitted.

"Think of that," he said. He made it sound as impressive as if I had walked. "You came all that distance to see my friend Manuel Maria?"

"Yes."

"To buy a painting, perhaps?" There was only the barest trace of irony in his voice.

"Not his paintings," I said. "But I am interested in his art. His praises are sung many places."

"It is true," he said solemnly. He looked around the street. There were three or four other persons in sight, but you couldn't say the Rua Fragoso was exactly crowded. "It is not wise to discuss business in the streets, Senhor. If you would care to come to my place next door …"

"Sure," I said.

I followed him to the place next door. It was a shop almost identical in appearance to the other one, but according to the sign this one was a wine shop. The old man opened the door and motioned for me to enter.

"After you, old one," I said. "I am a modest man. It would be unseemly for me to lead the way. And to turn my back on one of your years would be impolite."

He chuckled and stepped through the doorway. I followed. It was a small room, smelling of sour wine. There was one dim light. Enough to show that the room was empty except for us. There were two rickety tables, their tops stained with stale wine. On one wall there were a couple of shelves filled with dirty bottles.

"Some wine, Senhor?" he asked.

"No, thanks," I said.

He chuckled again. "You are wise, Senhor. It is not very good wine. Shall we put our heads to business?"

"Why not?" I asked.

"You are interested in the work of my friend Manuel Maria?"

"Yes."

He peered at me shrewdly. "It is not always easy to tell about the Americanos. But I think you are not of the police?"

"I am not of the police," I said.

"Good. Perhaps, then, Senhor, we can do business. I do the same work as did my friend Manuel. It is true that he specialized in making the documents of the countries of South America and that there were none finer at it. But next to Manuel, I am best, Senhor."

"I prefer to see Senhor Tristão," I said.

He spread his hands in an universal gesture. "I fear that is impossible, Senhor," he said. "Manuel is dead." His hand moved almost imperceptibly as he crossed himself.

That startled me. "How? Where?" I asked.

"The police discovered it only today. It is their belief that Manuel was murdered perhaps on Saturday last. They said they thought he may have been killed by one of his clients, but then he had so many clients, and by this time the murderer must be far away. Again, as the police say, Manuel was himself one who broke the laws, and too much regret is not to be expected. All of these things the police said as they stood over the body of my friend. I do not think, Senhor, that the police will look too hard for the murderer."

"How do you know all this?" I asked.

"It was next door," he said, indicating the wall. "And the walls here are thin." He paused, looking at me shrewdly. "The police are sometimes clever, Senhor. Manuel was murdered Saturday evening and he was killed by his latest client. A simple gunshot and Manuel was no more. I wept for his passing. We were business rivals, but he was also my good friend."

I glanced at the wall. "You heard him killed?" I guessed.

"Through this very wall, Senhor. It was known everywhere that Manuel never repeated a client's business, yet this was a client who did not trust even Manuel. He received his goods, paid for it as an honorable man, and then killed Manuel."

"Didn't you do anything to stop the killer?" I asked.

"But what was there to do, Senhor? Manuel was dead. I knew that such a one would not miss when he shot. It would not have brought life again to Manuel if I had rushed out to be shot in turn. I am saddened that Manuel is no longer with us, but business is business. Your needs, Senhor?"

I thought quickly. I had no doubt that it was Samson Carter who had killed the passport forger. It was part of the pattern which had included the man waiting at the hotel to kill any American who came searching for Carter too quickly. He was determined to reach the safety of his new life and to leave no tracks behind.

"Listen to me, old one," I said. "I do not want a passport. I have one already which will serve me well. ... In America, old one, I had a friend. He took something which was mine and ran away. I knew only that he would come here to see your friend, Manuel. I came after him as a man must when his honor is touched. My friend knew that I would be after him, so he arranged that I should be unable to come farther than the hotel. He sent a Senhor Carlos Sarmento to meet me."

"Carlos?" the old man asked. "You saw Carlos?"

"I saw him," I said.

"Fortune has favored you," he said, and there was respect in his voice. "Carlos is dead?"

"I do not kill boys when I am after a man," I said. "I do not need a passport, Senhor, but I will pay for what I do need."

"Also in little white diamonds?"

"No," I said. "In American dollars."

"I may have seen your friend," he said slowly. "There was another *americano* to see Manuel. He was a small one with eyes that looked at one without seeing. A small mustache, but newly grown. He also spoke Spanish as well as yourself. He came first on Thursday last."

"And his last visit was on Saturday night?" I asked.

"Perhaps," he said. "There is still, Senhor, the small matter of some business between us," he added almost apologetically.

"Of course," I said. I knew that the failure of Carlos was like a small insurance policy, but there was no point in pushing my luck. I put my hand in my pocket and pulled a single bill from the inside of my fold of money. The money was folded with the large bills inside. I put the hundred dollar bill on the table between us. "This one now," I said, "and four more like it when you have earned them."

He picked the bill up carefully between his fingers and examined it. "Truly," he said, "you are not of the police. A hundred blows they might give me, but never so many of the beautiful American dollars." The bill vanished. "It was your friend who was here on Saturday night."

"He shot Manuel?"

"Truly."

"What did Manuel make for him?"

"A passport, naturally," he said. "It was from the country of Argentina. As always with Manuel, it was a work of art."

"What name was on it?" I asked.

His shrug was an apology. "I do not know, Senhor. As I have said, Manuel did not talk of his business. It is only that I visited him when he was working on the seal of Argentina and recognized it."

"Do you know where my friend was going?"

"I am sorry, Senhor, no. The matter was not mentioned between them. The passport was finished on Saturday save for the photograph. Manuel had a camera in the back rooms and on Saturday night he took the picture of your friend. The first two did not satisfy your friend, but the third was to his liking. It was affixed to the passport and he paid Manuel in the small white diamonds. Manuel assured himself that they were genuine and then gave over the passport. It was then that your friend shot him and left."

"The wall is very thin," I observed dryly.

He grinned at me. "It is, Senhor. And when one places the ear next to it, it is of the ultimate thinness."

"What else?"

"That is all I heard, Senhor."

There was no reason to suspect him, yet I felt that he did know something else. "Well," I said, "many thanks." I started to get up.

"Senhor," he said in a pained voice, "there is still the matter of the remaining American dollars."

"If you had earned them," I said. "What you've told me isn't worth the advance I gave you. But I am a generous man, so you may keep it." I pretended I was going to leave.

"A moment, Senhor," he protested. "I merely said that was all I had heard, but I have not finished talking."

I sat down again. "I will listen," I said. "If your words are of value, they will be rewarded."

"Your friend," he said, "is very popular. There are others who wish to find him. Is it true, Senhor, that he possesses a great diamond, one that is a very grandfather of diamonds?"

"Where did you hear this?" I asked.

"Manuel," he said. "He always knew of such matters. The radio from America. Manuel listened often. On Thursday, after the visit of your friend, Manuel was telling me of a great diamond which had been stolen in America. Then, as he was telling me, he suddenly thought of something and he would talk of it no more. I think, perhaps, that it occurred to him that there might be a connection between the great diamond and his newest client. Is it true, Senhor, that the diamond is worth twenty million escudos?"

"That is a lot of money," I said. "I have never seen a diamond worth so much."

He chuckled. "It is not surprising so many are interested in your friend. If I myself were younger ..."

"What about the others who were looking for him?"

"On Friday there came two. Not together. The first one was a slim, elegant man who looked as if he had not slept in days. He was known to Manuel, who called him Senhor Lomer. He knew that the man he was looking for had come to Lisbon, and it seemed logical to him that such a one would have business with Manuel. But Manuel refused to tell him anything and he left. Later there came a *senhorita.* I did not see her, but I heard her. She was also known to Manuel, but he did not call her by name. She fared no better than the Senhor."

"Did they return?" I asked.

He shook his head. "Perhaps they did not find it necessary. I do not know, but if it had been myself, I would have found a way to watch Manuel's visitors. Or I might have watched the airport. Such a one would be in a hurry and would not take a ship when there were planes."

I nodded. If there were two persons already following Carter, then it was even more important that I follow him quickly. For all of Carter's thoroughness, he was still an amateur. It might not even occur to him that there would be others trying to steal the diamond from him.

"There was also a third person, Senhor." He looked at me slyly. "This one, perhaps, is worth even more of the dollars than you mentioned."

"I'll see," I said.

"This one came Saturday night. After Manuel was dead. I do not know his name, but I think perhaps he was of German blood. He was of about your own size and build, Senhor. His hair was blond and was trimmed short. There was a scar on his right cheek, like so." His finger traced an arc on his own cheek. "When he cursed softly to himself, it was in German. I think, perhaps, he had been to see Manuel before. When there was no answer to his knocking, he tried the door. It was unlocked and he went in. He seemed to know his way into the back rooms."

"The wall is truly of great thinness," I said sarcastically.

"A man lives by observing, Senhor," he said. "Your friend was a man of great care, but he made one small mistake. When he killed Manuel, he must have taken the extra pictures of himself. This was wise of him. But he overlooked the negative, which was hanging in the room where Manuel made the pictures. The blond man found this negative and took it with him. It was all he took, which is how I know he was interested in your friend. One thinks that he realized he could have a picture printed from the negative and show it at the airport and perhaps learn where your friend went."

"I have just had an interesting thought," I told him.

"I am listening, Senhor," he said politely.

"My friend paid Manuel in small white diamonds. Let us say the price was ten of them. Manuel was also holding ten small white diamonds which were to be paid to Carlos if he earned them. My friend did not take back the diamonds when he killed Manuel. If the door was unlocked, as you say, then someone who knew Manuel was dead might go in to make certain the diamonds did not go to waste. Such a one might be there to see another man enter. … When the police came, did they find any of the diamonds?"

He stared innocently back at me and shrugged. "Who is

to know what the police find," he said. "Or what they put in their pockets, for that matter. Not that I would begrudge them, Senhor. The living must live, for that matter. It is to be thought that wherever the soul of Manuel is"—his fingers again traced the pattern over his chest—"of a certainty he will not need diamonds."

He was right. If he had appointed himself heir to Manuel's fortune it was no business of mine. I had only been curious. "You are right, old one," I said. "Is that all you have to tell me?"

"It is all. One is not a bottomless well."

I reached into my pocket and separated five more bills. He had earned a bonus. I put them on the table and stood up. His gaze lingered for a moment on the pocket that the money came from. Caution was mixed with the regret in his eyes when he looked up.

"*Obrigado, Senhor,*" he said.

"*Não há de quê,*" I said. "*Adeus.*"

"*Bom dia,*" he said.

He was still fingering the hundred-dollar bills and gazing reflectively at my pocket as I left.

I went back along the Rua Fragoso, giving a wide berth to the narrow alleys that cut off from it every few yards. As soon as I reached a spot where I could find one, I hailed a taxi and directed him back to my hotel.

It was still early, but I didn't feel like sampling Lisbon night life. I told a bellhop to bring a bottle of brandy to my room and then I went on up.

I knew there was something wrong as soon as I entered the

room. For a minute I thought someone might be waiting there. But a quick look through the room cleared that up. I glanced around to see what it was that had disturbed me.

It was several minutes before I realized what it was. My suitcase had been moved. I went through it quickly. My clothes had been mussed up, but the only things missing were the description of Martin Lomer and the photograph and description of Samson Carter which Captain Gregory had given me.

The bellboy arrived with the brandy. I tipped him and poured myself a half-glassful. As soon, as the bellboy was gone, I picked up the phone and called the Polícia Internacional e de Defesa do Estado. It took five minutes to get someone who knew what I was talking about. Finally I got a man who knew there had been a call from the Aviz Hotel. But the man in the room was gone when they got there. The clerk had let him leave. When he learned that I was the Senhor March whose name the clerk had mentioned, he wanted to know if I could identify the man who had been in the room of the Senhor Carter. I said I couldn't and hung up.

So Carlos Sarmento was loose. I didn't think that he'd try to kill me again, but I'd keep it in mind anyway. I'd been mistaken before. What interested me more: was it Carlos or someone else who had gone through my room? My guess was that it wasn't Carlos. He might have taken anything about Carter, but there would have been no reason for him to be interested in Martin Lomer.

That left me with two choices. According to the old man on the Rua Fragoso, Martin Lomer had been on the trail of Carter.

But that had been on Friday. This was Monday. I was sure that Carter had already left Lisbon, probably the day before. If so, I doubted that Lomer was still around.

There was still the blond man with no name. He'd been in Lisbon as late as Saturday night. Maybe he was still there. And it was possible that he'd gotten curious about me. I didn't know how, but that didn't rule it out. With a diamond worth seven hundred thousand dollars at stake, the news was bound to sweep through the underworld as fast as if Malenkov suddenly visited the U.S. Senate. There might even be leaks that would tip someone off to my presence.

I was still trying to puzzle it out when I fell asleep.

I was up early the next morning. As soon as I'd finished my breakfast, I took a taxi to the airport. I checked first with Pan American. I showed them a letter I had from the New York Police Department, requesting that cooperation be given me. It was a little dividend that John Franklin had provided. It didn't carry too much weight, but it was enough for what I wanted. They let me see all their passenger lists for Sunday.

The passport forger had been killed Saturday night after delivering the passport to Carter. That meant that Carter would probably leave on the first available plane. I didn't know what name he would be using, but there was a chance I might spot it. Clever as he was, Carter was still an amateur and he was apt to make the mistakes amateurs make. So I especially looked for names with the initials S.C. or S.H.C.

I drew a blank at Pan American. I went over to the Iberia Airlines. It took them a little longer, but they finally decided to be impressed by the letter. Maybe it was the loan that

Congress made Franco. Anyway, they brought out the passenger list.

I hit pay dirt. On the Sunday afternoon plane to Madrid there had been a Señor Sansón Carrasco of Buenos Aires, Argentina. There could be no mistake about it. Carter's new passport had been from Argentina. The initials were S.C., and Sansón is the Spanish version of Samson. And just by luck, I remembered something else. Sansón Carrasco was a minor character in *Don Quixote*. I'd had a period, years before, of being crazy about the book, and I remembered that Carrasco was the Bachelor in the Second Part. It was the Bachelor who brought Don Quixote and Sancho the news that their adventures had been put in a book, supposedly written by an author named Cide Hamete Berenjena.

The next plane to Madrid was that afternoon. There was an empty seat. I bought a ticket and went back to the hotel to check out.

Knowing that they kept track of everybody who entered or left, I stopped by to say good-bye to the police. I complimented them on their astuteness in the case of the late Senhor Carter and told them I was going on to Madrid for a few days' vacation before returning home. The less they knew about it, the less they'd want to stick their noses in. We separated with a barrage of compliments and everybody was happy.

When the Madrid plane took off that afternoon, I was aboard. It was a short flight, but I had a copy of the Lisbon *Diário de Notícias* and a paperback Spanish edition of an

American mystery—*La Cosecha del Verdugo**—to help me pass the time.

I had just settled down to read the mystery when I glanced at the passenger who sat across the aisle from me. He'd been buried behind a newspaper since we took off, but it was lowered. He saw me looking and quickly raised the paper again, but not before I'd seen him. He had short blond hair. And there was a scar on his cheek in the shape of a half circle.

---

* The title translates literally as "The Executioner's Harvest"; this is clearly a reference to the author's *Hangman's Harvest* (1952), the first book in the Milo March series. I have found no evidence that *Hangman's Harvest* was published in Spanish, so this could possibly be a private joke of the author's.

INTERLUDE 3

He had gone straight to the Palace Hotel when he arrived in Madrid. He had never been there before, yet he had pored for many hours over the plans of the hotel so that he knew it as if he had lived out his life in the building. He knew the exact room he wanted. On the sixth floor. In the rear. And he knew what could be seen from the window.

It could be arranged. A boy took him to the room and showered startled thanks on him for the tip of twenty-five pesetas. He listened impatiently and waited for the boy to leave. At last he was alone. He left his bags in the center of the floor. He glanced around at the quiet luxury of the room and felt the first calm touch of security.

He walked to the window and looked out. His gaze went directly to the street as though this were not the first time he had seen it. The Calle de Cervantes. From the first time he had learned there was a street called Cervantes, he had known he would get a room from which he could see it.

He turned and walked back into the room. He stood in front of the mirror and looked at himself. The new mustache was already a thin black line across his lip. But that was not the only change in his face. The lines of tense determination were gone, with only shadows to mark their passing after twenty years. His face was soft now. And somehow he seemed bigger.

"Señor Soltero Sansón Carrasco," *he said aloud,* "que opina usted acerca de eso? … Vaya con el mozo! Muchas felicidades!"

At the sound of his voice, he could feel the last vestige of Samson Hercules Carter slipping from him. It was almost a physical act. There was a fleeting moment when he thought the mirror showed the shadowy figure of Mr. Carter leaving one side while from the other side Señor Carrasco stepped confidently into his place.

He smiled at the reflection of his new self. "Le suplico a usted que me perdone," *he said. He went over to sit on the edge of the bed.*

He took the blue diamond from his pocket and looked at it.

He could still remember the first time he had seen a diamond of any size. Light had flickered within the stone and he had been lost. He had known immediately that his life was somehow linked to diamonds. There was a purpose to his life. The next day he had gone to the doctor and told him there would be no further visits.

At first he had thought only in terms of diamonds of three or four carats. His ambition had been to own as many of those as he could. He lived as cheaply as possible. Half his remaining money went into diamonds; the other half he saved. He'd made no friends. Friends cost money and they offered him less warmth than the diamonds. He'd lived only for the day when he'd go to Spain to live.

Then came the day when he'd seen his first really big diamond at the House of Stones. The diamonds he owned turned to glass. He continued to buy the small ones, for it gave him a reason for visiting Robert Stone, but they meant no more than the money he was saving. Then, in turn, all other diamonds ceased to have meaning once he had seen the Tavernier Blue. He'd held it in his hands and watched the shifting light inside it. He'd had the feeling then, and reexperienced it each time he looked at it, that there was something inside the diamond. Always he felt that he was on the verge of seeing what it was—then it would slip away from him in the changing light. When that happened, he was always overcome with the sense of loss.

The Tavernier Blue had been a turning point in his life. Once he had seen it, his drive to own it had become an obsession. He existed on one dream—the day when the Blue would belong to him. It was then that the character of Señor Sansón Carrasco began to take form in his mind—a secret personality, hidden carefully. The world around him was a place of quiet terror. He knew better than to reveal any of his plans.

He'd bought the gun and practiced in his room, without benefit of shells, until he was certain he knew how to use it. He was determined to protect his rights. The business of the passport had been sheer inspiration. He had seen the story in the newspaper and had immediately gone to the prison to see the man. From that time on, his plans ripened quickly.

He had permitted himself only one luxury. He smiled as he thought of it, for it had been something which Sansón Carrasco could appreciate even more than Samson Carter. He hadn't needed the help of George Harder; it was seldom that Robert Stone wasn't called to the phone while he was there, and all he had to do was wait for such a time. But he had endured the jibes of George Harder for fifteen years, and it had amused him to involve George with the police.

Señor Carrasco stared feverishly at the stone in his hand. Once more he thought he was about to see what was in the heart of the diamond. His breath came faster and there was a sudden dryness in his mouth. Light moved in the diamond like a live thing. It shimmered and shifted, and his eyes ached. He put the diamond away, covering the fire that was never still. Perhaps tomorrow he would see what was inside the stone.

"Donde menos se piensa, salta la liebre," he said, shrugging gently.

Señor Sansón Carrasco left his room and went downstairs to the glass-covered patio. There was just time for a glass of manzanilla before the siesta hour.

SIX

The plane came down over the Barajas airport, nine miles north of Madrid. From the air it looked like a toy city sprawling over its plateau, then it expanded rapidly as the plane went down. It vanished from view as our wheels touched the ground.

I waited long enough so that I left the plane directly behind the man with the scarred face. I stuck close to him as we lined up to have our luggage checked. I let two people crowd in between us, but that was all. He was careful not to look at me. It was a safe guess he had an idea we were both looking for the same person. Maybe he was the man who had gone through my room in Lisbon.

There was a limousine waiting to take the plane passengers into Madrid, but scar-face ignored it. He stopped in the waiting room and took a long time to light a cigarette. He was checking on me, so I went out to the limousine. When I got there, I doubled back and found another entrance.

He was standing at a telephone. As I watched, he finished the call and started to make another one. I guessed that he was doing some of my preliminary work for me. I went back out and found a taxi. It was an old, beaten-up American car. A Buick. It looked like it had the life expectancy of a match, but there weren't any that looked better.

The driver leaped out and opened the rear door while I was still several yards away. He bowed so low I couldn't help wondering if it was only an excuse to see if his car was still in one piece.

"I want to go to Madrid," I told him, "but not just yet." I climbed into the back and sat down. "We'll wait a few minutes."

He looked his question without saying anything.

"There will be another man out of there in a minute," I said. "He'll probably take a taxi. I want to follow him without him knowing anything about it. Think you can do it?"

He looked interested but not too much. He spread his hands in a futile gesture that belied the eagerness in his eyes. "It would be a matter of difficulty, Señor," he said. "As one can see, my car is of a great age. He does not always go well." He watched me slyly.

"Would a hundred pesetas help your car to go well?" I asked. I wasn't being as reckless as it may have sounded. That was about two bucks at the tourist rate of exchange. "In addition to the meter fare," I added.

His face lighted up. "Señor," he said fervently, "for one hundred pesetas my car will put on wings and follow a bird if that is your desire."

"I don't think that will be necessary," I told him. "I'll tell you when he comes out."

"Visto bueno," he said cheerfully. That's about as near to "okay" as you can come in Spanish.

It was another fifteen minutes before he came out. He picked one of the taxis nearer to the door. When it pulled past, I was glad to see that it didn't look any stronger than the one I was sitting in.

My driver pulled out of the line when the other taxi was a couple hundred yards away. As we hit the main highway into Madrid, he let another car squeeze in between him and the other taxi. I decided he knew his business and settled back against the seat.

The lead taxi didn't seem to be in a hurry and we were about thirty minutes reaching Madrid. Then we wound through the narrow streets of the old section and soon hit the center of the city. I noticed that there were still a few scars from the civil war, but most of the ruined sectors had been rebuilt.

We drove along the Calle de Alcalá and turned into the Paseo del Prado. Ahead of us, the other cab pulled to the curb.

"He is stopping at the Palace Hotel, Señor," my driver said.

"Wait to see what he does," I said. "If he dismisses the taxi, pull up when it leaves."

My taxi eased into the curb and we watched. The blond man climbed out and started talking to his driver. It looked to me as though he were arguing about the fare. It must have seemed the same to my driver.

"Alemán," he said with scorn. "Spain, Señor, is filled with these blond ones from Germany. Since the war they have overrun Spain like cockroaches, and one would think they owned us. It is to our shame."

I couldn't resist a little thrust. "I thought Generalissimo Franco has said that there are no Nazis in Spain."

The back of his shoulders shrugged with eloquence. "Generalissimo Francisco Paulino Hermenegildo Teódulo Franco

Bahamonde," he said, rolling the name over his tongue with subtle mockery, "is a Galician." He paused a moment. "It is said that Galicians are sly like lizards. When they say yes, in their hearts they are saying no. ... He is going in, Señor."

A uniformed man had come out of the hotel and picked up the German's luggage. As soon as they vanished into the hotel, my driver pulled up in front of it. I got out and handed him a hundred and sixty pesetas.

"Gracias. Vaya usted con Dios," he said. "Señor, you are staying in Madrid?"

"For a while," I said. A bellboy came out of the hotel and stood at attention. I nodded and he started taking my luggage out.

"You will have need of a taxi," he said. "You will ask for Bernardo Goma, Señor? Everywhere in Madrid they know me. And I will make it my pleasure to be near the hotel often. If it is things you wish to see, then I am your man. The Prado, the Plaza Mayor, Retiro Park, the National Palace, the Plaza de Colón—"

"I'm not much of a tourist," I said.

He glanced at me shrewdly. "Then you may wish to follow another taxi as you did today. You will find, Señor, that I am a man of talents. Bernardo Goma. You will remember the name?"

I laughed. "I'll remember your name, Bernardo."

"Le agradezco mucho su amabilidad," he said. He clashed the gears and the old Buick lurched away.

I turned and followed the bellboy into the Palace Hotel. My German was not in evidence in the lobby. He had apparently registered and been taken to his room. I signed my name to a register card and pushed it across to the room clerk.

"As I was coming in," I said casually, "I thought I saw a friend of mine arriving. A Señor Carvalho. A tall, blond man, with a scar on his face."

"There was such a gentleman," the clerk said. "But I fear it was not your friend. The gentleman was a Señor Rainer Eckholdt from Germany. He phoned earlier from Barajas to make the reservation."

"I had only a brief glimpse of him," I said. "I thought he was my friend, but I was mistaken."

The clerk was feeling sociable. "An understandable mistake, Señor March. But it would have been most amusing if it had been your friend. The Señor Eckholdt wouldn't make a reservation until he was sure that *his* friend was staying here."

"Ay, qué risa," I said gravely. "There are many Germans staying here?"

"But his friend is not German," the clerk said. "His friend is a distinguished visitor from Argentina. A Señor Carrasco."

"It's a small world," I said brilliantly. I was feeling pretty pleased with myself. The German had led me right to Carter. I had expected him to.

"It is truly said that Madrid is becoming the hub of the world," the clerk said proudly.

"Don't let Boston hear you say that," I told him.

"Perdón?"

"A local joke—and not a very good one." I turned to the boy who was holding my luggage. *"Vámonos."*

"Voy, Señor," he said.

We made a small procession across the lobby to the elevators.

"Seis," the bellboy told the operator.

We slid up to the sixth floor. I followed the bellboy out and back along the carpeted floor to 612. He unlocked the door and bowed me in.

It was a nice room. It was going to cost Great Northern five bucks a day. I gave the boy a five-peseta note and waved him out. I unpacked my things and sat down to think things over. Now that I'd found Carter, one of the first things to do was to call New York, but that would have to wait. It was noon in Madrid, but it was only six in the morning in New York.

It was a little risky, but I decided to call the operator and find out what room he was in. I lifted the receiver.

"What room does Señor Carrasco have?" I asked the girl who answered.

"Six-nineteen," she said. "But Señor Carrasco is not in now. He will be back at siesta time."

"And what time is that?" I asked.

"Four o'clock, Señor. You wish to leave a message?"

"No message," I said and hung up.

It was too good a chance to pass up. Carter was on the same floor and only a few doors away. I got up and looked at my door. The lock was a cinch to pick.

I opened the door and looked out. The corridor was empty.

I went down to 619. I knocked, just to make sure. There was no answer, so I went to work.

It took me less than a minute to pick the lock. I stepped inside and closed the door behind me.

The room was very much like mine. Carter had been in it only two days, but there was already an air of neatness about it that was his own personal stamp.

I checked the windows first. There was one opening on a fire escape. I threw the window up. If he came back early, I'd have a way out. Then I went to work on the room.

I didn't find much. He'd replaced the clothes he'd left behind in New York and Lisbon. Except for a few things that had been bought in Lisbon, they were all from Madrid shops. Not the sort of clothes that a tourist would have bought. Everything fit in with the taste of a middle-class European. Carter had taken a long step toward becoming the character he had imagined for himself.

In one drawer I found several small diamonds, each one carefully wrapped in tissue paper. They certainly represented only a small percentage of his collection of stones. I couldn't see any obvious reason why he had them tucked away— unless it was mad money, the way a woman will sometimes slip a few dollars in the sugar bowl.

In another drawer I found his gun. It was a .32 with a two-inch barrel. This was probably the gun he'd used to kill the guard in New York and the forger in Lisbon. The gun had been carefully cleaned and wrapped up in a new handkerchief. There was a box of shells, each one neatly in place, wrapped in a separate handkerchief. I couldn't shake off the impression that these things had been put away as a man stores something which he never expects to use again. It was as though Samson Hercules Carter had needed a gun, but Señor Sansón Carrasco couldn't possibly need one.

The dual personality of Carter was quite unlike anything else I had ever encountered, yet I understood it—and was fascinated by it. It wasn't only his changeover from one personality to the other; it was more the combination of shrewdness and innocence with which he had done it. Here was a man who had planned and executed one of the cleverest crimes in years. He had planned every step with such precise care. He had killed unemotionally when he felt it would help to cover his tracks. In a general sense you could say he had been brilliant; but he had overlooked things which a child could have seen. And once he'd arrived at his hideout, he'd automatically assumed it was all over.

He'd been in Madrid only forty-eight hours, yet already two of us were in the same hotel with him. Rainer Eckholdt and I. There were two others after him—Lomer and a girl—and maybe they had traced him. And I was sure that this had never occurred to Carter.

I went over the rest of the room—everything, even the water tank in the toilet. I poked through a jar of shaving cream, smoothing it over again when I was finished. I covered every inch of that room, but there was no sign of the big diamond. I hadn't really expected to find it—he probably wore it next to his heart—but I'd wanted to make sure.

I checked the room to make sure that everything was the way I'd found it. I looked out in the hallway. Then I closed the window and left his room.

I spent the next hour in my own. I knew better than to try to get lunch in Madrid before two o'clock. Finally, a few minutes after two, I went downstairs. I had some manzanilla and langostas, which is cold lobster. Then I had coffee and some more manzanilla while I listened to the conversations around me. They weren't worth listening to. The Palace dining room was filled with tourists, most of them Americans.

Nothing can make an American so anti-American as running into his countrymen in Europe. Most of them thought everything in Spain was quaint. The others couldn't wait to get back to dear old Keokuk. They complained about the dining hours. They thought the Spaniards lazy because of the siesta and they complained because everything closed up from four to six.

When I couldn't stand any more of it, I went out to the lobby. I stopped to pick up a paper. There wasn't much choice. I could read a paper with a Royalist slant, or the Catholic view, or the Falangist. I took *Arriba,* the Falangist paper. Then I retired to a comfortable chair from which I could see most of the lobby.

There wasn't much worth reading. Every other story was a sales talk on how much Franco was doing for the people of Spain, or how he was outsmarting the crafty foreigners. Since he had tricked Congress into giving him several million dollars, maybe they were right.

I tried the society page. It, at least, was more amusing, but it sounded as if the editor had tried to crowd in the names of everyone listed in the *Anuario Español del Gran Mundo.* Franco's name was generously sprinkled through it, too. The Generalissimo had entertained at his country home. So had General Alfredo Kindelán y Duany. A Señor Javier Sanjurjo was off to San Sebastian. There had been a big party at the Valencia estate of Johannes Bernhardt. It mentioned that Bernhardt had been the president of the Sociedad Financiera Industrial, but it neglected to add that he was one of the top Nazis still in Spain. I guess they thought it wouldn't be polite to point.

Finally I turned to the ads. There wasn't much that the censor could do about the Banco Central having two hundred million pesetas in circulation.

It was about 3:30 when I saw Eckholdt come in. I made myself inconspicuous behind the paper. There was a scowl on his face, so I guessed he'd been looking around without much success. He made a quick survey of the dining room, the American bar, and the patio. Then he went upstairs.

It was only a few minutes before four when Carter came in. He didn't look much like the photograph the cops had given me, but still I would have recognized him anywhere.

Less than a week ago Samson Carter had stolen the diamond, but he had changed so much that I doubted if many of his old acquaintances would have recognized him. It wasn't only the mustache. His face had changed. The photograph had shown a tension in his face—a familiar look in the faces of most Americans. That was gone now. His hair was longer in the back. The clothes were part of it, too. In a subtle fashion the man who had a week before looked like thousands of other Americans now looked like a thousand other Spanish gentlemen.

But that wasn't the most astonishing thing. I'd trailed a lot of men. Until now, I'd never seen one who could forget that somewhere there were people looking for him. It would show in the way their eyes would quickly check every room they entered. But not Carter. There was nothing but innocence and an air of belonging in his attitude.

He talked for a minute to the clerk, then he went upstairs. It was siesta time. If Carter was going to be the Spanish gentleman, he'd certainly be out of circulation for the next two hours. I went up to my own room and stretched out on the bed.

It was almost six when I awakened. I took a shower, changed clothes, and went down to the American bar. It was coming to life again.

I hadn't been there long, nursing a glass of manzanilla, when Eckholdt came in. I became interested in the arrangement of the bottles back of the bar, watching him in the mirror. He did a quick check of the room but didn't see me. Then he went to the other end of the bar. He ordered a drink, but he wasn't interested in it. He was watching the entrance.

Carter came in a few minutes later. He looked around and then went to one of the tables. It was occupied by two Spaniards. They seemed to know Carter, and he joined them.

Eckholdt spotted him, all right. He watched Carter in the mirror. As soon as it was obvious that Carter was settled for a while, he pushed his glass away and left the bar. He sauntered slowly out.

I had a hunch. I waited about five minutes and then followed. I took the elevator to the sixth floor. The corridor was deserted. I went past my own room and stopped in front of 619.

After a moment I heard it—a slight rustling beyond the door as though the room were overrun with mice. Only this time it was a rat. I put my hand on the doorknob and twisted it gently. It was unlocked. I turned it carefully as far as it would go. Then I threw it open.

He was going through the dresser. He heard the click of the latch and whirled around, his hand sliding into his coat pocket. He recognized me, but the only sign of recognition was the darkening of the scar on his cheek.

"Ich bin beschäftigt—" he began. He broke off, hesitated uncertainly, then switched to bad Spanish. "What is the meaning of this intrusion? I am busy. You have made a mistake."

Now I was certain that he was the one who had been in my room in Lisbon. In some way he had discovered that I was following Carter and had gone through my things to see what I knew. But there had been nothing to show that I represented the insurance company. Now he was unsure of himself. He didn't know whether I was the law or merely more competition.

I stepped farther into the room. "I'm afraid it is your mistake," I said. "What are you doing in my room?"

It threw him off for only a second. "Your room?" he said harshly. "Come, Herr March, what is your game?"

"You know my name?" I pretended surprise. "That should help prove that you deliberately broke into my room."

The fact that I was talking to him convinced him that I was not from the police. The conviction made him bolder. It also made him angry. The scar was a dull red.

"Stop it," he said. "What's your game?"

"No game," I said. I continued to move closer to him. "But you're wasting your time here, Eckholdt."

"You've got it?" he asked quickly.

I shook my head. "But I've already covered this room. The Tavernier Blue isn't here."

I laughed.

"There's enough in it for both of us," he said. "I've got contacts."

"So have I."

"The minute I get my hands on that diamond," he said, "I've got a buyer for it." His face was sharp with greed.

"When you get your hands on it," I said. "Some guy who'll give you ten percent of what it's worth and then cut it up and make engagement rings out of it?"

"No," he said. "This is a collector who'll buy and no questions asked. I talked to him before I even started. He'll pay a half million. Two hundred and fifty thousand apiece."

"We both know there can't be many collectors like that. Maybe I can find him myself. I don't think I want to play, Eckholdt."

His eyes hardened. "I could make you."

"How?"

He started to jerk the gun from his pocket. That was his first mistake. I hit him. He crashed against the dresser. The gun went off, the bullet thudding into the carpet. Smoke curled up from the hole in his pocket.

He was off balance and I had enough time to measure him for the next one. I caught him across the base of the jaw and his eyes went glassy. His knees buckled and he slid gently to the floor.

I crossed the room and picked up the phone.

"I just caught someone trying to break into Room 619," I said. "You'd better ask the manager to come up with a policeman." I replaced the receiver.

The shot had already attracted attention. I heard voices out in the hallway. A moment later a couple of people looked cautiously around the edge of the door.

It didn't take them long to arrive. I heard the elevator door bang and a moment later they bustled in: the assistant manager of the hotel walking solemnly behind the dignity of his office, the *guardia* mentally tugging his uniform into greater neatness, and finally, a man with the past in his eyes.

Señor Sansón Carrasco had retreated enough for Samson Carter to look out through his eyes. He had realized that strange men in his room might mean a threat to his diamond. When I first saw him, I had a sudden hope that the threat might make him reveal something. But all I learned was that the Samson Carter who twice had killed was not far beneath the surface of the Spanish *don*. His gaze flickered quickly to the drawer where his gun was put away. Then it came back to settle on me with a searching wariness.

"*Dios mío,*" exclaimed the assistant manager. His hands drew excited diagrams in the air as he turned to Carter. "I assure you, Señor Carrasco, that such things do not happen here. It is—"

"*No se afane tanto,*" the policeman told him. He pulled a

notebook from his pocket and looked at me. "Señor, it was you who telephoned?"

"Yes," I said. I was acutely aware of Carter's gaze fixed on me. The important thing was to convince him that he had succeeded in leaving the past behind.

"Señor," the policeman said gently to remind me that it was my story.

"Lo siento muchísimo," I said. "My name is Milo March. I am across the hall in 612. I was just stepping out of my room when I saw this man breaking in here. I grabbed him. He put up a little fight and I'm afraid I had to knock him out."

"You are a guest in the hotel, Señor?"

"Yes. I arrived today."

"From America?"

"Yes," I said. Carter was paying more attention to my replies than the policeman. "From Denver, Colorado."

"You speak our language well, Señor," the *guardia* said graciously. "The purpose of your visit?"

I could feel Carter's intensity. "A vacation," I said. "I've always been fond of Spain, although I haven't been here for several years. But what does that have to do with this event?"

"It is unusual for guests to attack robbers," the policeman said.

"He means," the assistant manager put in hurriedly, "that it is unusual for guests to have the opportunity to attack robbers."

I laughed. "I guess I didn't think," I said. I tried to sound a little more like an American tourist. "I guess I've always been used to taking care of myself, and when I saw this man breaking in, I just came after him without thinking."

"He was already in the room?" Carter asked.

I looked at him as if I'd never seen him before. Then I turned back to glance at the policeman and the assistant manager.

"This is Señor Carrasco," the assistant manager said. "It is his room."

"Señor Carrasco," I said. He gave a little bow in return. "The thief was inside the room. He was already at your dresser. It is obvious that he is a mere sneak thief."

"How did you know it wasn't his room?" he asked. He must have realized that this was a leading question, for he gave a little laugh. "You will pardon my curiosity, Señor? It is that I would have assumed that a man entering a room had the right to be there."

"Sure," I said. "But I never heard of a man picking the lock to his own room."

He nodded thoughtfully. The wariness retreated a step.

"One more question, Señor," the policeman said. "As we left the elevator, one of the guests mentioned hearing a shot. Do you know anything of this?"

"Yes. There's a gun in his pocket. He was trying to pull it when I grabbed him. It went off in his pocket. The bullet went into the carpet."

"*Válgame Dios,*" the assistant manager said. His gaze searched the carpet, his hands weaving their pattern of woe.

The policeman made a few more notations in his notebook and put it away. He turned to Carter. "You will make charges, Señor?"

"Well," Carter said uncertainly, "if nothing has been taken—"

"I will make charges," the assistant manager said excitedly. "I will—"

The assistant manager had been too worried about the hotel property. The policeman had been interested in me. So had Carter. And I'd been watching Carter. We'd all forgotten about the German on the floor.

I don't know when he recovered, but he made his break while the assistant manager was talking. He rolled to his feet in one swift move and leaped for the doorway. The guests in the hallway scattered like fire in a high wind.

I caught him just as he reached the door. I grabbed him by the shoulder and whirled him around. That would have been enough, but I couldn't be sure that he wouldn't say something about the Tavernier Blue. He could babble all he wanted to when they got him to the police station, but I didn't want that diamond mentioned here. I held him off with my left hand and slashed him across the jaw as hard as I could.

He staggered across the hall until the wall stopped him. Then he folded to the floor. That German certainly had a glass jaw. The innocent bystanders came surging back to stand by.

"De un golpe lo derribó," one of them said. *"Vaya con el mozo!"*

I grinned at my admirer and turned back to the room where the three men were still in various stages of flat-footedness. "He's all yours," I told the policeman. "Better pick him up while he's still portable."

"Thank you, Señor," he said gravely. He couldn't decide whether to be grateful or annoyed.

"Do you require me further?" I asked.

"No, Señor. Perhaps at the hearing. ... You will be available?"

"When will the hearing be held?"

The *guardia* shrugged. From what I'd heard about Spanish prisons, that was the right answer. I grinned and turned to the other two. "Good afternoon, gentlemen," I said.

"Señor March," the assistant manager said, "the management is grateful." He managed the difficult feat of putting gratitude into his voice while making it imply that I should have been more careful of hotel property in bringing about the capture.

"I am also grateful, Señor March," Carter said. The suspicion had gone entirely and he was once more the portrait of a Spanish *don.* "I trust I will have the opportunity to repay you."

"Es algo trivial," I said. *"Adiós."* I walked down the hall to my own room.

I waited until I heard the hallway clear. Then I picked up the phone and put in a transatlantic call to Great Northern in New York. After about ten minutes of static and the fading voices of operators, I got John Franklin.

"Milo here," I said. "Madrid is the end of the trail. But don't mention any names." I wasn't sure, but I had an idea that somewhere in Spain there was somebody keeping in touch with phone calls out of the country. I didn't mind if they got interested in me as long as they didn't know anything about the Tavernier Blue.

"Fast work, Milo," he said. "Any trouble?"

"Not for me. But there was a man in Lisbon who gave a good impersonation of the guard in New York."

I wasn't sure whether he whistled or it was static.

"There's one problem," I continued. "I've been through his things. No sign of the rock. Maybe it's on him and maybe it's stashed away somewhere. You want him brought in, or you want me to play games?"

He thought about it for a minute. "From our angle," he said, "the stone's the important thing. You'd better try to locate it before you move in on him."

"Okay. What about the New York cops?"

"I guess I'll have to tell them," he said heavily. "I'll try to talk them into letting you play the hand. But maybe they'll insist on sending somebody. If they do, I'll tell them to have him contact you."

"You'd better send me some more money," I said.

"All right." He sighed. "But you'd better come up with a miracle, boy. The stockholders are going to have high blood pressure when they see the size of your expense account."

"How could you tell they were executives if they didn't have high blood pressure?" I countered.

"Seen any competition yet?" he asked.

"Some," I said. "Lomer was in Lisbon. Haven't seen anything that looks like him here yet. There was also a girl looking around in Lisbon. Then there's a third one. Ever hear of Rainer Eckholdt?"

He thought about it a minute. "Yeah," he said finally. "He's an ice man. I don't think he's ever worked over here. Mostly in Europe. But he's a top man. I think they want him in Paris. He there?"

"Yeah. He just made his first play and I caught him out at

first base. He's in safekeeping. I'd hate to think he had the chance to talk to the wrong people. If he's wanted in Paris, why don't you call them and tell them to ask Madrid for him. All that's against him here is breaking and entry."

"I'll do it, Milo. Anything else?"

"That's about it," I said. "Send the money to the Palace Hotel. Make it a couple of thousand so I won't have to stint myself."

"What the hell are you trying to do—buy Franco?" he growled.

"No spikka da English," I said quickly and hung up. Maybe he thought it was all right for him to make cracks about Franco, but I was the one in Spain. And I wanted to get out. I hoped that whoever was tapping the phone had been napping.

In a way I was glad he wanted me to find where Carter was keeping the diamond before he was pulled in. I didn't like the idea of cops trying to beat it out of him.

After the business of Eckholdt, I'd probably have no trouble getting friendly with Carter. In one way that would make it easier; in another it would make it harder. I wouldn't be able to trail him. I'd have to work out some way of checking on him when I wasn't around.

The next step would have to wait. I couldn't press the advantage too quickly. I put the whole thing out of my mind and went out on the town.

SEVEN

The following morning I had breakfast in the hotel and then walked down Carrera de San Jerónimo until I came to the Puerto del Sol. I had no trouble finding the police headquarters—the Dirección General de Seguridad. It was a huge building, complete with its own prisons, right on the Puerto del Sol. On top of the building there was a large clock that was supposed to show the correct time.

Inside, I cooled my heels for a while and finally some official decided to see me. He examined my passport as if he expected to find a Spanish Republican under the seal. Finally he grunted and made out a resident visa for me. It gave me the right to stay in Spain for three months. That ought to be long enough. Anyway, they'd ask too many questions if I applied for the Autorización de Residencia para Extranjeros.

It was still early, so I got busy on one of my chores. I checked the banks that were near the hotel. For the time being I skipped the little banks and concentrated on the branches of the Banco Hispano Americano, the Banco Central, and the Banco Español de Crédito. I found out there was a new account at the Banco Central in the name of Sansón Carrasco, but no safe deposit box. It was the latter I was interested in.

On the way back I stopped in a shop on the Calle de Alcalá

and bought a box about the size of one you'd keep jewels in. I had it wrapped in plain paper. Then I went on to the hotel.

I told the clerk I wanted to see the assistant manager. After a moment he came bouncing out. The same guy who'd showed up the day before. I guess he'd finally decided it wasn't my fault that the German shot a hole in the rug, for he gave me a big grin.

"Ah, Señor March," he said. "A pleasure! I know, of course, that you are an American, but March is a famous name in Spain. Are you related to our Don Juan March?"

"Juan March Ordinas?" I said. "I'm afraid not. Our ancestral bloodlines are several million dollars apart."

"*Ay, qué risa,*" he said, but he didn't laugh as though it were funny. "What can I do for you, Señor March?"

"I wondered if you'd put this in the hotel safe for me," I said, extending the box.

"*Claro que sí,*" he said. He hefted the box and was impressed by its lightness. "Valuables?" he said.

"In a way," I answered, truthfully enough. I hesitated long enough to make it casual. "I suppose after the incident of yesterday that Señor Carrasco has also put all of his valuables in your safe, too."

"No," he said. He struggled with discretion and it lost. "Señor Carrasco consulted us and upon our advice made arrangements with a bank."

"His diamonds, too?" I asked casually.

"I do not know, Señor. He asked us for the name of a good diamond house and we recommended La Onza de Oro." His tone said it was none of my business. I grinned back at him as if it were and waited while he scribbled out a receipt for my package of valuables and affixed half of it to the package.

I went looking for La Onza de Oro—"The Ounce of Gold." It was on Calle de Zaragoza, not far from the Ministry of Foreign Affairs. I was shown into the manager's office. The manager and I spent the next half hour exchanging compliments. When we'd run out of things to flatter each other about, we got down to business.

Yes, Señor Carrasco had brought in some diamonds for sale. Very fine quality, little white and blue diamonds. He was a little cagey about the price, but finally told me that he had paid Señor Carrasco approximately one and a quarter million pesetas for the diamonds. That was about twenty-five thousand dollars at the tourist rate of exchange.

We agreed that Señor Carrasco was a great gentleman, that Madrid was the most wonderful city in the world, and that the weather was superb. It was understood that if I ever had any need for jewelry or souvenirs of Spain, I'd come to La Onza de Oro. In return for this the manager developed a serious concern for my health and the health of my family. Finally I managed to tear myself away. Doing business in Spain was like going to put the touch on a maiden aunt.

I walked over to Calle Mayor and headed back toward Puerto del Sol. I hadn't learned much, although I had eliminated a few possibilities. He had apparently sold all of his small diamonds except for the few I'd seen in his room. He'd made no move to sell the big diamond. He hadn't put it in the hotel safe. Unless he'd picked on one of the smaller banks, he hadn't put it in a safe deposit box. I was certain it wasn't in his room. That left only my original guess: he must be carrying the diamond on him.

It was almost two o'clock. I decided not to go back to the hotel. I'd stop off at one of the street cafés in Puerto del Sol and have lunch. Then, later, I'd casually manage to run into Carrasco. I was startled to realize how thoroughly he had changed over to his new identity; I was thinking of him as Carrasco rather than Carter.

The Puerto del Sol was alive with activity. The cafés were already crowded and there were a lot of people standing or strolling on the street. The sidewalks were teeming with beggars, peddlers, and bootblacks. Most of them were children—small, undernourished kids with intense faces, looking older than their years. I had a pocketful of five-céntimo coins and I carefully gave one to each beggar. Not to give something to a street beggar in Spain is to bring a hundred curses down on your head.

I was about to cross over to one of the cafés when I saw a dozen kids clustered around a man. The man was Sansón Carrasco. As I drew nearer, I saw the reason for their interest. I watched as he held up his right hand with a single golf ball held between thumb and forefinger. He waved his hand languidly and there were two golf balls. He took the second ball and put it in his pocket. He waved his hand again and once more there were two golf balls.

The children were enthralled. They were watching intently as the balls continued to multiply. There was one exception. A small, sharp-faced boy, with bootblacking equipment slung over his shoulder, stood near Carrasco and only half pretended to watch. I suspected that he was trying to pick Carrasco's pockets.

I waited on the edge until the little man glanced up. "Hello," I said, deliberately using English. "That's quite a trick."

It wasn't acting; by this time he had so thoroughly become Sansón Carrasco that there was no need for acting. He looked at me as if he'd never before heard English. *"Qué es eso?"* he asked.

"I am sorry," I said switching back to Spanish. "Sometimes I forget. I was merely remarking on your sleight of hand. *Magnífico."*

"It is nothing," he said. He closed one hand around the golf ball and blew on the clenched fist. Then he slowly opened his fingers. The ball was gone. He glanced up and the expression on his face reminded me of a small child who has just tricked his elders. "It amuses me."

"You perform well," I said.

He shrugged. He pulled some coins from his pocket and handed five céntimos to each kid. "And for you, *chico,"* he said, turning to the boy I had noticed, "ten céntimos—after you have returned the golf ball you took from my pocket."

The boy grinned impishly and handed over a golf ball. He took the coin and tested it with his teeth. Then he faded away with the others.

"I am glad to see you, Señor March," Carrasco said, turning back to me. "I have not yet properly thanked you for your kindness of yesterday. Will you honor me by dining with me tonight?"

"It will be a pleasure," I said.

"Excellent. Shall we say at ten, Señor March? At El Púlpito. Anyone can tell you how to find it. Until then, Señor." He nodded his head in a birdlike gesture and walked briskly away toward our hotel.

I was surprised that he had made the first friendly move. Then I realized that such a gesture was in keeping with the role he had assumed. Probably, too, he felt some compulsion to test his new role with a fellow American.

I waited until he was out of sight. I looked around at the kids. One of them came hurrying over.

"Shoeshine?" he asked in English. "I say the English," he added proudly.

"Pues sí," I agreed. "I want a shoeshine, but not from you. I want that one over there." I pointed to the boy who had been picking Carrasco's pockets.

"Tiene mucho pico," he said, weighing his chances of talking me out of my choice.

"So he's a chatterbox," I said. "I like chatterboxes. He is the one I want." I tossed the boy a ten-céntimo piece.

He caught it deftly and turned to shout at the other boy. *"Oye, tú!* Ernesto!"

The other boy heard him. He walked slowly, eying me with speculation. It was easy to read his thoughts. It was an honor to be singled out; it was also something to arouse suspicion.

He was probably about ten, although he was no larger than a boy of seven or eight. His clothes, clean but ragged, hung on his skinny frame in a way that told they had been handed down, perhaps for generations. The olive skin of his face was drawn tight over the cheekbones so that his eyes seemed overly large, like two chunks of coal. His black hair hung over his forehead, and he kept brushing it out of his eyes with an impatient gesture. The expression in his eyes was that of a weary, cynical old man.

"Señor?" he asked warily.

"Shoeshine," I said, indicating my shoes. They were already brightly shined, but he said nothing. He dropped to one knee and went to work. His hands flew swiftly and automatically over my shoes, but I could tell by the way he held his head that he was waiting for my pitch. I let him wait.

When nothing happened, he made his own pitch. "Some new shoelaces, Señor?" he asked. His tone implied my own were mere shreds.

"No, thank you," I said.

"Perhaps, Señor, you would like to examine some fine razor blades."

"No."

He tried again without varying the rhythm on my shoes. "Some excellent hand soap, Señor? It cannot be obtained in the stores because the shameless authorities will permit none that is not made by their own kind. But I swear by San Isidro—"

"No soap," I said firmly.

He looked up out of those young-old eyes. "Girls, Señor?"

I shook my head.

A different look came over his face. "Boys, Señor?"

I laughed and he bent over my shoes again.

As he finished the second shoe, he lifted my foot and tugged at the heel. "It is a little loose, Señor," he said.

The shoes were new and the heel wasn't loose, but I merely grunted.

He held my foot so I wouldn't feel the pressure and twisted the rubber heel off. He held it up triumphantly. "You see, Señor? Loose."

"It does seem loose," I had to agree.

"But do not worry, Señor," he said happily. His hand dived in among his things and came up clutching another heel. "It will be like new."

I waited until he had fixed the new heel to the shoe. He turned to look with speculation at my other shoe, but I moved my foot. He sighed in defeat and stood up.

"That will be twenty-five pesetas for the shoeshine and seventy-five for the heel, Señor," he said.

I shook my head. "Ten pesetas for the shine and thirty pesetas for the heel," I said, quoting what I knew were the current prices.

He stared at me until he decided there was no point in arguing. Then he grinned suddenly and held out his hand. I put the forty pesetas into it.

"Now," I said, "stay and talk to me a moment and I'll give you another forty pesetas."

He looked at me shrewdly. "So, Señor?"

"What's your name?"

"Ernesto."

"Ernesto what?"

"Ernesto Pujol, Señor."

"You look like a bright boy, Ernesto," I said. "Why is it that you were able to get only a golf ball from that man's pocket earlier and to be caught doing even that? It was clumsy of you."

He stared at me searchingly and I grinned. He grimaced, looking for the moment like a shrunken gnome. "It was easy to find what he had," he said. "In one pocket his money— much money—a Don Dinero he is. In another the céntimos he likes to hand out. In a third his golf balls. Another pocket some thimbles like a woman might carry. In still another his passport and his residence visa. That was all. But when I tried to reach the pocket which held his money, he always moved. Then I took the ball in anger."

I was conscious of the inventory he'd made. "Are you sure that was all he had on him?" I asked.

"Before God, Señor," he said. "I thought even of a money belt, but he had none." A new look came into his face. "You are interested in the gentleman's pockets, Señor?"

I was still thinking about what Ernesto had said. The diamond was large enough to have been felt by a clever pickpocket, and I was sure the child was clever. The shape of the diamond made it impossible that he might have confused it with one of the golf balls. Yet if it wasn't on him, where was it?"

"Señor?" he asked patiently.

I realized what he had asked. "No, Ernesto," I said, "but I am interested in the man. ... How would you like to earn two hundred pesetas a day for a while?" I could have hired him for half of that, but I didn't see any reason why I should save Great Northern's money for them.

He tried to look like a gangster in an American movie. "You

want me to take care of him?" he asked. From somewhere in his ragged clothes, he produced a switchblade knife with a cracked bone handle.

"No," I said quickly. The knife vanished. "I want you to watch what that man does every day. Each day, when you report to me, I will give you two hundred pesetas. Okay?"

"*Visto bueno,*" he said. I could see that he was already imagining himself as a sort of Castilian Humphrey Bogart. "Where shall I report, Señor? At your hotel?"

"Better not come to the hotel," I said. "I'll meet you here every day about this time. Don't let him know you're watching him."

"Don't worry, Señor," he said confidently. "I shall be as invisible as the wind from the mountains of Guadarrama."

I laughed. "*Adiós,* Ernesto."

"*Espere un momento,*" he said. "You are forgetting something, Señor."

"What?"

"A matter of forty pesetas, Señor. For talking with you." I pulled out forty pesetas and handed it to him. "Anything else, Ernesto?"

"How are you called, Señor?" he asked. "It is so I will know the name of the *caballero* for whom I work."

"You mean so you'll know who to look for if I don't show up," I told him. "It's Milo March. And I'm living at the Palace Hotel. But don't worry, Ernesto; I'll show up to pay you."

He grinned at me. "*Sé bueno,*" he said impishly. "Be good." He turned and swaggered over to the other boys. He handed his equipment to a smaller boy who looked enough like him to be his brother. He responded to the excited questions with an air of mystery. He walked away. I watched him until he vanished down Carrera de San Jerónimo.

Then I crossed the street to the nearest café.

Most of the street tables were crowded, although there were a few with but a single occupant. The waiter led me to such a table. The man who sat there was perhaps in his fifties. His hair was white, as was his close-cropped mustache, his clothes were neat and clean, but when I looked at them closely I could see they were badly frayed. I was reminded if the old Spanish proverb: "An honorable gentleman goes ragged rather than patched."

He was sipping a glass of *tostado,* a cheap drink made from grapes, but not exactly a wine. There was a small plate of canapés in front of him. I had an idea that this was his sole lunch.

It was easy to look at him and guess his whole history. He was one of Spain's poor rich, almost a professional caste. Spain is really ruled by the group known as the Oligarchy, or the Family, consisting of about five thousand persons. About half of them own most of the wealth. They are, of course, the ones who actively rule, with Franco as their manager. But there are several hundred members of the Family who have nothing but their connections. They have no money, yet they can't bring themselves to take jobs. They exist by grace of being in the *Anuario Español del Gran Mundo* and the favors they can get through their connections.

The waiter took me to the table and pulled out a chair, but I waited until the older man looked up. "Your permission, Señor?" I said.

He was surprised, but he recovered quickly. He stood up, making a little bow. "I am honored, Señor," he said.

We sat down. I looked up at the waiter. "Manzanilla," I said. "What do you recommend for lunch?"

"Paella or bacalao," he said. Both were casserole dishes, the first a wonderful—when properly cooked—concoction of clams, chicken, shrimp, and veal cooked in rice, while the second is codfish.

"Where does your chef come from?" I asked.

"Valencia."

"Then I will have paella. One moment," I added as the waiter started to leave. I turned to the man across the table from me. "Señor, I am a stranger in your country. Since I have intruded on your table, will you do me the great honor of having lunch with me?"

He had a brief struggle between pride and hunger, but I had phrased it so that he could accept. The latter won. He also ordered paella and I told the waiter to bring a bottle of Marqués de Murrieta with it.

When the waiter was gone, I smiled at my companion. "Milo March," I said.

He managed a little bow even sitting down. "Don Raimundo Agustín y Ramos Salamanca," he announced. I'd been right. Anyone with a name that long in Spain comes from an important family. If the poorer Spaniards gave their children such long names, they'd run out of names long before they ran out of children.

The waiter brought our manzanilla. I raised my glass. *"Salud y pesetas,"* I said.

"*Salud,*" he responded.

We drank. Manzanilla is a wonderful white sherry from Andalusia. It is bottled ambrosia, but it sneaks up on the unwary.

He complimented me on my Spanish and wanted to know where I was from. I told him.

"America?" he said. He seemed to be surprised. "You like our country, Don Milo?"

"I like your country very much," I said. There was no point in explaining that I liked Spain but didn't care for the Oligarchy, and even less for Franco. I would hurt the old boy's feelings and he'd give me a long lecture on how Spain was different. I'd heard it often, sometimes even from Americans. In Spain it usually ran, "Democracy is a social attitude, not a political one, and the Spanish people want it that way." But I could never find anyone who could prove that anybody had ever asked the Spanish people.

"Most Americans don't," he said, explaining his surprise. "We Spanish are not normal. We have breakfast at ten in the morning and no one of importance gets to his office before noon. Then lunch is from two to four, with two hours to recover. Then work from six to ten in the evening. But you Americans live under the illusion that you like to work."

"Not me," I told him. "If I had a large enough income, I'd be satisfied with a diet of good food, wine, and women."

"A *señorito?*" he asked with a little smile.

I looked my question.

"According to José Antonio Primo de Rivera," he said, "*señorito* is the final decadence of *señor.* He used it to describe those of us who have no profession—only a taste for good food, good wine, bad women, bullfights, and café gossip, with the income to afford all of these things."

"The income disqualifies me," I said lightly. "What is your opinion on the matter, Don Raimundo?"

He smiled without humor. *"El escarabajo llama á sus hijos granos de oro,"* he said. "The black beetle calls its young ones grains of gold."

The waiter arrived with the paella and served it. I tasted mine and it was wonderful. The waiter nodded at the expression on my face and left.

"You see," Don Raimundo said, "I have given another example. In Spanish one can say nothing so beautifully that a man would have to devote his life to it to be certain that nothing had been said."

He was right. I laughed.

"Look about you, Don Milo," he said, waving his glass of wine. I think, in a sense, he was putting on a show to repay me for the lunch. Yet he was perfectly sincere. "We are in Madrid, where the air from the Guadarrama Mountains will not so much as flicker a candle flame, yet it will kill a man with the disease of the lungs. Spain is filled with uniformed robbers and ragged beggars. If we have trouble with foreigners, we know it is because they do not have the good fortune to be Spanish. In Spain there is no middle way; people are either brilliant like me or dull like everyone else."

"Sounds like a comfortable attitude," I said. I was enjoying myself and I had no intention of disputing him.

"Perhaps," he said. He hung there on the edge of the new sentence until he was sure I was going to let him continue. "We Spaniards are more honest than other men, Don Milo. Have you ever noticed that even our language is not a normal one? It is so much better than other languages. Let us take the word *señorito,* which Don José used to describe those of us who are above professions and work. When the word first strikes your ear, there is a feminine ring to it, is there not?"

I agreed that there was.

"That," he said triumphantly, "is as it should be. In any other language the name would be an insult; in Spanish it is a subtle compliment. In our dictionaries, Don Milo, *la gente* and *el pueblo* both mean 'the people.' But only in the dictionaries. In usage the feminine noun *la gente* means the nice people; the masculine noun *el pueblo* means the masses. So even in trying to insult us, Don José paid us the compliment of admitting that we are *la gente.*"

I thought that was cutting it pretty thin, but I only grinned and let him go on. Which he did all through lunch.

He was still at it when the waiter brought coffee and cognac. "We Spanish," he said, "always expect the unexpected. Have you heard the latest joke going around the cafés?"

"I don't think so," I said.

"Don Milo, have you experienced our Spanish trains?"

"Not this trip. But I've been on them. You mean they are no better?"

"Worse, Don Milo. … Recently it was announced that El Caudillo obtained the loan from your Americans because of fear of the aggressive Russians. But around the cafés they are saying the Russians only think they can invade us; they don't know Spanish trains."

He threw back his head and laughed. It wasn't as funny as he was making it out to be, but that was all right. He laughed so loud he couldn't hear that I wasn't laughing.

He went on talking while I leaned back and stared off at the Guadarrama Mountains. The sky was a clear blue with a few lacy clouds frilling it.

I decided it was time to break off the conversation. It was amusing, but I'd had enough for one day. I mumbled something about the weather and caught the eye of a newsboy. He came over and I bought a copy of *ABC.* I turned to the weather report, not really caring but following through.

"You wish to learn the weather forecast?" Don Raimundo asked.

"Yeah," I said. "I have a dinner appointment tonight. ... Ah, here it is. Continued fair and warmer tonight."

"Don Milo," he said in a confidential tone, "it grieves me to say this, but our newspapers cannot always be trusted. You wish to know what the weather will be like, I will find out for you. Come."

"Don't bother," I said.

He stood up. Until then I'd been thinking of him as a rather pathetic figure, but now he was changed. He had taken on a new dignity; he was a man with a purpose. "No bother, Don Milo," he said. He smiled. *"Enchufe."*

I knew about *enchufe.* Literally it means the plug by which an electrical appliance is connected to a power system. But most of the time when you hear it used in Spain, it won't mean anything electrical. It will mean pull or connection. Those who have Family membership, no matter how distant, have *enchufe*. By this time I was curious to see Don Raimundo's *enchufe* operating on the weather. I followed him inside the restaurant.

Don Raimundo picked up the phone and put in his call. He identified himself to someone he called Don Estebán. For ten minutes they discussed the health of various relatives. Finally Don Raimundo got around to asking the name of the director of the government weather bureau. It took him another five minutes to say good-bye.

He made his second phone call. He went through three or four people, patiently requesting to speak to Don Luís Arrese. At last he was speaking to Don Luís. He introduced himself—Don Raimundo Agustín y Ramos Salamanca, friend and cousin of Don Estebán María Paulino y Aranda. There was more conversation about Don Estebán and then he asked about the weather. Three more minutes of parting remarks. Then Don Raimundo hung up and triumphantly reported.

It had taken only twenty-five minutes for Don Raimundo's *enchufe* to get the weather forecast. Continued fair and warmer. Just like it said in the newspaper.

It was almost the siesta hour, so I didn't have too much trouble saying good-bye to Don Raimundo. I promised to meet him again. I meant it, too. While I'd been amused by his method of learning about the weather, I knew it wouldn't hurt to cultivate him. There might be a time when his *enchufe* could be put to better use.

I paid the bill and went back to the hotel.

Ernesto was just leaving the front of the hotel as I arrived. He carefully looked all around before he consented to recognize me.

"I am on the alert, Señor," he said. "I will be back here before the end of the siesta. Since the gentleman is Spanish, he will not stir from the hotel during the siesta."

I didn't bother telling Ernesto that the gentleman wasn't Spanish; he was giving such a good imitation he probably wouldn't think of breaking the siesta. I didn't intend to break it myself.

I stayed in my room through the siesta. But I didn't take it as easy as I'd intended. I got to thinking about the diamond and that was the end of any rest. It seemed silly that a diamond almost as big as a golf ball and worth seven hundred thousand dollars could suddenly become invisible. It hadn't been deposited in the hotel safe. There was no safe deposit box in the name of Carrasco; he seemed to have no fear of being followed, so I was certain he would have rented a box in the same bank where he opened an account if he had wanted one. I had covered his room without finding the diamond. Ernesto had the same results from covering his pockets.

Remembering what Robert Stone had said about him, I was sure he would keep the diamond where he could look at it often. The question was, where?

I went downstairs later. I didn't feel like sitting around in the bar, watching the tourists get loaded. I went down San Jerónimo, crossed Puerto del Sol, and walked up Calle de Hortaleza until I reached Avenida de José Antonio. There were several movie houses there. I finally settled for an old Abbott and Costello picture, with a Spanish soundtrack.

It was almost ten when I came out. I found a taxi and told the driver to take me to El Púlpito.

The restaurant was a small one, slightly off the regular tourist beat. I had never been there, but I remembered reading about it. It was reputed to have once been the hideout of Luís Candelas, the Castilian Robin Hood—having been operating in the same spot since the eighteenth century. Because of that, it drew a few tourists, but most of them prefer the bigger and brighter spots.

I dismissed the taxi and went in. It was a small restaurant, filled with the tantalizing blend of aromas. I soon saw why. The cooking was being done at one end of the restaurant where you could see the whole operation.

He was waiting at one of the tables. He stood up as soon as he saw me, a smile on his face.

"There you are," he called. "I am glad to see you again, Don Milo." He had decided to be very friendly.

"Hello, Don Sansón," I said. We sat down and I glanced around the restaurant.

"You have not been here before?" he asked.

"No."

"I think you will like it," he said. "The food is magnificent. Would you care for a drink?"

"Manzanilla," I said.

He nodded his approval and beckoned the waiter. He ordered a bottle of manzanilla for us. The waiter treated him as if he were an old customer. I was suddenly aware of how much he was enjoying this, completely aside from his possession of the diamond. It was a way of life for which Samson

Carter had sacrificed everything so that Sansón Carrasco could enjoy it. And sitting there opposite him, I found it hard to realize that this was the man who had carried out a clever robbery and murdered two people.

"There is nothing quite like the manzanilla of Andalusia," he said. "You must have spent some time here, Don Milo."

"Several years ago," I said.

"But this time you have only recently arrived?"

"Yesterday." I wondered why he was pumping me. I was sure that he didn't suspect me.

The waiter brought the manzanilla and we toasted each other.

"I have always been interested in your country," he said. He glanced at me slyly. "You know I am also an American."

I didn't have to pretend to be surprised—I was. Surprised that he mentioned it. But luckily I didn't say anything.

He chuckled. "South American," he said. "I am from Buenos Aires, Argentina. I have been here for only a few days myself."

"I would have taken you for a native of Spain," I murmured.

He was pleased. "Most do. Of course, I am Spanish, even though my family has lived in South America for many generations. But tell me about North America, Don Milo. Where is it you are from?"

"Denver, Colorado."

"Ah, yes. You flew to Spain?"

I nodded.

"By what route?"

I decided to leave Lisbon out of it. There was no point in

pushing my luck with too many coincidences. "I have always preferred coming by Paris," I said. It was true. I would have preferred it.

"New York to Paris," he said. He raised his glass. *"Salad y Nueva York."*

We drank to health and New York.

"I have read so much about New York," he said, making it sound truthful. "It has always seemed such an exciting city— always something happening, and, of course, the crime. The city of gangsters. But then America is famous for her gang- sters."

I felt myself getting annoyed. It was strange. It was the sort of remark I might have made myself. Normally, if another American had said it, I wouldn't have minded. But I would have been annoyed to hear a Spaniard say it. I was accepting his disguise so well that I was reacting as if he were Spanish.

"I suppose so," I said. "But the only difference between America and, say, Spain is that over here the gangsters are the government."

He wagged a forefinger at me. "Careful, Don Milo."

"What's wrong?" I asked. "Afraid that a Falangist will over- hear us and you will be in trouble for listening to me?"

He didn't answer immediately. He glanced at his watch and smiled. "It is almost time," he said. "They should be along any minute. In fact I think I hear them now. Listen."

I listened and after a minute I heard the sound of music from the street. It was very faint but growing stronger. Someone was playing an accordion and three or four persons were singing. It was another minute before I could distinguish the words.

Francisco Franco no sabe gobernar,

Y sus ministros le siguen la corriente.

No, no, no, no, Francisco Franco, qué no, qué no!

The voices and the music faded away up the street. Roughly, the translation of the song was "Francisco Franco doesn't know how to rule, and his ministers follow the line of least resistance." It wasn't the sort of song I expected to hear on the streets of Madrid. My surprise must have shown in my face, for he chuckled.

"I am told," he said, "that there is an official policy permitting this sort of thing. In certain quarters you will also hear considerable grumbling about Generalissimo Franco. It is good for people to blow off steam. It is understood, of course, that should the complaints become organized or take on a more political nature, the police might step in."

"Of course," I said dryly.

"Still," he said, "I don't believe that it is wise for a stranger in Spain to be careless about his remarks. That is why I suggested that you be careful, Don Milo."

He was more right than he knew, I suddenly realized. I resolved to keep off the subject of Franco and the Falange.

"You are right, Don Sansón," I said. *"Le agradezco mucho su amabilidad."*

"Es algo trivial," he answered. He leaned back and lit a cigarette. It was an American brand, but even that was not out of keeping, since the Spanish who could afford to do so invariably smoked American cigarettes. Having tried a few Spanish brands, I didn't blame them.

"Yes," he continued, "I have always been fascinated by the stories of crime in New York. Tell me, Don Milo, you must have been in New York about a week ago—were there any especially interesting crimes in the papers while you were there?"

Then I knew why he had started questioning me. He shared at least one trait with other criminals; he was anxious to know what was being said about his crime. That probably explained why he had become so friendly on such short notice. Once he had convinced himself that I had no interest in his diamond, he saw me as a possible pipeline. There were American newspapers to be had in Madrid, but he probably wouldn't risk buying one.

"Can't think of any," I said. "But, of course, I've never been much interested in crime."

"What is your profession, Don Milo?" he asked.

"I'm interested in rocks," I said. I deliberately used the word *pena,* which means a large stone, instead of the more common *roca.* I thought it was too bad he couldn't appreciate the pun.

He looked puzzled. "A geologist?" he asked.

I grinned. "You might call me that," I said. "I do a lot of digging around."

"I've heard it is an interesting occupation," he said politely. "Shall we order, Don Milo? I think you will find all of the food here is excellent."

I nodded and he beckoned the waiter. He ordered *angulas,* baby eels served with a very special sauce, and recommended them to me. But I was going to have enough trouble just watching him. I ordered *gazpacho,* a cold raw vegetable soup, and *tordos* with wild asparagus. *Tordos* is thrush served on a spit. Even before I tasted them, I decided I'd have to come back because they'd look wonderful on an expense account.

When they came they were so good that for the moment I was in the frame of mind to say to hell with the Tavernier Blue.

"What about you, Don Sansón?" I asked while we were eating. "Are you here on a vacation?"

"No, I have retired," he said. "I intend to live in Spain."

"In Madrid?"

"Oh, no. I shall stay here for a month or two. Then I shall go to a small town about twelve miles north of here—Alcalá de Henares. I intend to buy a small house there."

"Since that is the birthplace of Cervantes," I said, "it should be the perfect place for the Bachelor, Sansón Carrasco."

I thought it might make him suspicious, but there was only bright interest in his eyes. "You recognized my name?" he said in delight.

"Sure," I said. "Sansón Carrasco, son of Bartolomé Carrasco, recently made a Bachelor by the university at Salamanca, who brought Don Quixote the news that his adventures had been put into a book. But as Sancho said, 'The tail is yet to be skinned. All so far has been tarts and fancy cakes.' "

He beamed at me. "This is most startling," he said. "You are the first one to recognize my name since I arrived in Spain. I have found it rather disappointing."

"I'm sure," I said.

"My father," he continued, "was a great admirer of the *Don Quixote* novel. When I was born my father heard my howls even before someone could arrive to tell him that he had a son. Claiming that I myself had been the first to bring him the news that his earlier—ah—adventure had finally taken tangible form, my father insisted on naming me Sansón. He was a man of great wit." He beamed at me again.

I wondered if it had taken him twenty years to think up that explanation of his name. It was one, I was sure, which would delight any Spaniard who was familiar with *Don Quixote.* There was an almost authentic ring to it. Except for the grammar, it might have come from the lips of Sancho himself.

The waiter came and took away the empty dishes. We ordered wild strawberries, coffee, and two glasses of *anís.*

"Were you an only child?" I asked. I suspected that, if pressed, he could have as easily provided the history of three or four generations of the mythical South American Carrascos. I had no intention of pressing him that far.

"Ah, yes," he said. He smiled as though at some secret joke. "I'm afraid that thereafter my father emulated the tailor of El Campillo."

I knew the secret joke. It had to be one of the rhyming proverbs from *Don Quixote. "El sastre del campillo, qué cosía de balde y ponía el hilo,"* I said. "The tailor of El Campillo who threaded his needle and stitched for nothing."

He laughed with delight. "This is wonderful, Don Milo," he said. "I, of course, came to share my father's love for Cervantes, but it is not often that I meet one who knows the story as well as you seem to. It was a good wind that blew the thief into my rooms so that we might meet."

As I was to discover again and again, his fantasy had

become so real that there were times when I was in danger of being pulled into it myself. I had to concentrate to keep remembering that this was not a South American gentleman whose father had loved Cervantes and instilled that love in his son. I had met many murderers, but never one who was so innocent after the fact.

So, over coffee and *anís,* we talked about Miguel de Cervantes and his stories of Don Quixote. The more he talked, the more I saw that this Sansón Carrasco was just as much the creation of Cervantes as the first one had been, although the author had been dead for three hundred years. His idea of a Spanish gentleman was taken from the Cervantes book. Just as Don Quixote had so thoroughly believed himself a knight that his cardboard helmet became the finest ever made and his sway-backed drayhorse became equine perfection, so had he constructed the personality of a Spanish gentleman that was more real than Samson Carter had ever been.

I remembered what the psychiatrist had said about Carter's emptiness; how he had to take all of his values from outside himself. He had taken his from a book.

I wondered what part the great blue diamond played, since he retained just enough reality not to display it openly.

It was after one o'clock when we left the restaurant. As we waited on the sidewalk for a taxi, I saw a pale face watching us from the shadows. It was Ernesto.

As our taxi pulled away from the curb, I turned to look through the rear window. I was curious as to how Ernesto would follow. I saw the small figure dart from the shadows at the last minute and cling to the back of the taxi.

INTERLUDE 4

"Qué descanse bien," *he said to the American as they parted on the sixth floor. It had been a pleasant evening and he felt in the grip of a strange exhilaration. It was almost like being drunk, but he'd had very little to drink.*

His hand shook a little with eagerness as he put the key in his door. He knew why he had to hurry, and suddenly he was convinced that tonight he was going to see what was imprisoned inside the diamond.

He stepped inside, switching on the light. He closed the door and locked it. Without waiting to remove his hat, he uncovered the secret hiding place of the diamond, letting the light plunge into the deep blue fire. He held it in his hand, partly shielding it with his other hand so that only a thin beam of light struck the diamond. It darted to the very center of the stone, where it split into a dozen rays, each flashing off on its own tangent. It was like watching a rain of fire.

He removed his hand and let the full glare of the light fall on the diamond. The glare diffused as it entered the stone, softening to a pale blueness. It seemed to gather in the center of the diamond, where it swirled like smoke in a glass.

His throat was tight as he bent over his cupped hand. It seemed to him that he could see a face forming in the heart of the blue flame, and he knew that the next minute he would see who it was. He could hardly breathe as he waited for the face to become solid.

The tension became too much for him, and his hand shook. The light shook and shattered—lancing off toward every facet of the diamond. The face was gone.

He knew it was gone. He put the cover back over the diamond and tightened it. He felt a great sadness weighing him down; it was familiar, but he couldn't remember why.

He barely had the strength to remove his clothes. He turned out the light and got into bed. He bunched the covers up around one hand and shoved it against his mouth. He drew up his legs until they rested comfortably a few inches from his chest. Then he went to sleep.

EIGHT

It was almost lunchtime the following day before Sansón Carrasco came downstairs. He walked listlessly across the lobby. He looked as if he'd had a bad night. I timed my exit from the bar so that I met him halfway across the lobby. Accidentally, of course.

"Don Sansón," I said, giving my best imitation of surprise. "How are you this morning?"

"I am well, thank you, Don Milo," he said, but he didn't sound as if he meant it.

"I was just about to walk over to the Puerto del Sol and have lunch," I said. "Will you do me the honor of being my guest?"

He wasn't too anxious, but he could hardly refuse without being impolite, so he finally accepted.

As we came out of the hotel, Ernesto was waiting, keeping out of reach of the doorman. As he saw us, he ducked around that official and came impudently up to us.

"Señor," he said to me, his voice filled with mock humility, "a few pesetas, for the love of God. My mother is ill, there are many mouths to feed in our house, and my father gave his life for the Glorious Movement."

Under cover of giving him a few céntimos, I told him where we were going. He turned to Carrasco and repeated his request for money. When he had it, he thumbed his nose at the doorman and scampered down the street.

In honor of Carrasco's mood I suggested taking a taxi. One pulled up and we climbed in. I told the driver where we wanted to go.

It was only a short drive to the café where I had lunched the day before. We were silent until we got out of the cab and were going to a table.

"I'm afraid I'm not very good company today," he said.

"We all have days like that," I said. "A glass of manzanilla and you will revive."

"Que Dios le oiga," he murmured.

We found an empty table and ordered manzanilla. A bottle. I noticed my guest of the day before once again seated at a table with a small glass of *tostado* before him. I told the waiter to bring us a third glass and to ask Don Raimundo to join us. Carrasco looked surprised but said nothing.

In a moment the other man came to our table.

"Cómo se encuentra usted, Don Raimundo?" I said. "I would like to present my friend Don Sansón Carrasco. Don Raimundo Agustín y Ramos Salamanca."

The two of them uttered polite phrases while they carefully inspected each other. But it wasn't long before they were warming up. I had expected they would. Don Raimundo represented to a large degree what Carrasco wanted to become, while the latter was already a good enough imitation to be acceptable. Under a generous application of Spanish gentility, Carrasco began to come out of his mood. An equally generous application of manzanilla undoubtedly helped.

I saw that Ernesto was already across the street with the

other boys, who were busily drumming up whatever business they could. I said something about wanting a shoeshine and excused myself.

Ernesto saw me coming. He grabbed a blacking box from another kid—the one who looked like his brother—and was there to meet me when I reached the sidewalk.

"Shoeshine, Señor?" he asked with a grin.

I nodded. "Anything to report, Ernesto?" I asked as he went to work.

"Nothing of importance, Señor. After the siesta hour yesterday, the Señor went to the Royal Palace in the Plaza de Oriente. By the use of great cunning I slipped past the guard and followed him inside. But all he did was go to the Banquet Hall, where he spent all of his time looking at the curtains. There were pictures on the curtains—pictures of some *hombre* as long and skinny as a Barcelona sausage. The *hombre* was riding a horse, a very crow of a horse with a sway back and a belly that hung down like that of a woman with child."

"Don Quixote," I said.

He shrugged his thin shoulders. "I do not know his name," he said, "but he must have been a hungry one. If the Señor wanted to see hungry ones, he could have gone home with me. But he stayed there all afternoon staring at the *hombre* on the curtains. When he left, he went straight to the restaurant where you met him. Last night he did not again leave the hotel once you had returned there. I watched, Señor, until his light went out. I was back there early this morning, but he did not leave until he came out with you a few moments ago. I'm sorry, Señor, but that is all."

"Are you sure you didn't leave something out?" I asked him. "I want to know every little thing he does."

"He went once to the toilet as he was leaving the Palace and he stopped once in the Plaza de España to show some children the trick with the golf balls. Is that what you wish to know, Señor?"

I nodded. "That sort of thing. If he speaks to someone, if he stops in at a store to buy something, every little thing."

He looked surprised. "You want me to continue watching the Señor?" he asked. He had evidently been afraid that he was going to lose a good thing.

"Yes," I said.

He grinned and stepped up the rhythm of his polishing.

"Ernesto," I asked curiously, "what are you going to do with the two hundred pesetas a day I'm paying you? That's a lot of money."

"Not so much, Señor," he said. There was an old expression on his face as he looked up. "I take it home. There are many hungry mouths there—more than there is money to feed them. There is Antonio, Andrés, Roberto, Inés, Josefina, Enrique, Rosalía, Luisa, and Ignacio."

I whistled. "Who's the oldest?"

I am," he said with pride.

"And how old are you?"

"Ten years, Señor."

Ten years old and he had nine younger brothers and sisters. I was trying to think how to phrase the next question when he spoke again.

"Then," he said, "there is my mother and my father and my father's older sister, Tía Ana."

"Your father?" I said. "But a moment ago in front of the hotel you said that your father gave his life for the Glorious Movement—whatever that is."

He grinned up at me. "When one is asking for money, Señor, it is profitable to have a sick mother and no father. And if one says that the father died for the Glorious Movement, it is still more profitable. You understand, Señor? If the person is a Falangist, he may assume that my father died for the Falange and give a little more; if he is a Republican, he will assume that my father died on the barricades of Madrid and give more."

"Doesn't it bother you to lie so shamelessly?" I asked.

"A otro perro con ese hueso," he said scornfully. "Give that bone to another dog."

I laughed. "You are right, Ernesto. It is a bone and for a dog, which you are not. Tell me, Ernesto, how much do you usually earn?"

"Fifty to a hundred pesetas a day, sometimes more, sometimes less," he said with pride. "There are many men who do not make more than twenty-five pesetas a day on their jobs."

"I know," I said. I looked at his thin frame and knew the next answer, but I asked it anyway. "How does your family manage?"

He shrugged. "This way and that. There is always the black market. If there is not enough money, it can still be done. For one week we can not eat our potato ration and sell it on the black market, then use the money to buy bread on the black market. It is easy. ... Perhaps, Señor, you think El Caudillo rules Spain?"

"Doesn't he?"

"Por supuesto que no! Don Dinero rules Spain, Señor. If you have enough money you can buy the whole government."

"What about your father? Does he work?"

"No, Señor. My father has not worked in twenty years."

"Why?"

For the first time he looked around to be sure that no one could overhear us. And when he spoke, his voice was low. "My father comes from Estremadura. There he was a terrorist. He worked with El Campesino and El Degollado. During the war my father was a Republican. When the war was over, he was in prison for three years. He has not been bothered since then, but the Sindicados will not permit him to work anymore." He put the last touch on my shoes and stood up.

I counted out two hundred and ten pesetas and handed it to him. But I was still curious about this half-child, half-man.

"Ernesto," I said, "do you know what you want to do when you grow up?"

"Yes, Señor," he said coolly. "When my brothers are old enough to support my mother, my father, and Tía Ana, I will become an anarchist."

"Communist?" I asked.

He shook his head violently. "Señor, I spit upon the Communists. Ask my father. The war would not have been lost but for the Communists. They wanted to destroy everyone but themselves. La Pasionaria, I spit upon her. Uribe, Cordón, Galán—I spit upon them all, dogs that they are." He spat on the ground. "I will be an anarchist. El Mensajero de Muerte."

The Messenger of Death. He'd been sounding very adult until that last sentence. But then I remembered that some of the leading Spanish anarchists had taken names just as childish. I suppressed my grin.

"I'll see you here tomorrow, Ernesto," I said.

"Hasta muy pronto," he said with a quick grin.

I walked across the street to the café. Carrasco (I never thought of him as Carter now) and Don Raimundo were mellowed by constant applications of manzanilla and were engaged in a friendly quarrel over who had the greatest influence on fifteenth-century Spain, Isabella of Castile or Cardinal Ximenez de Cisneros of Toledo.

We had lunch. They continued their talk, but I joined in no more than I had to. Ernesto's Spain was too close for me to find much interest in the Spain of Don Raimundo.

After lunch I paid the bill and left them still talking at the table. I went back to the hotel until the siesta was over. Then I located Bernardo, the taxi driver I'd had the first day, and started out. I wanted to check on something, and I had decided to test Ernesto's theory that Don Dinero ruled Spain.

He was right. I had no trouble finding a customs official who was willing to enlarge his supply of pesetas. For one thousand of them I learned that a man named Martin Lomer was in Spain. He had arrived, by air from Lisbon, on Monday. He carried an English passport. He was staying at the Ritz Hotel, just across the Paseo del Prado from the Palace. I had no doubt that this was the same Martin Lomer, the international jewel thief, that the New York cops had told me about. The same Martin Lomer who had been asking questions of Manuel María Tristão in Lisbon.

For a minute I was tempted to go see Lomer, but I dropped the idea. It might expose me. My best bet was still to cultivate Carrasco. That way, if Lomer did make a move, I'd be there to stop him.

During the next five days I spent most of my time with Carrasco. We did the town, Carrasco with all the eagerness of a tourist but with more aplomb. We looked at the architecture of the Puerte de Toledo and the Puerta de Alcalá. We admired the roses in Retiro Park. We saw so many churches I started seeing stained-glass windows in my sleep. We spent an hour in silent admiration of the statue of Cervantes in the Plaza de las Cortes and a good two hours with the statues and stone reliefs of Don Quixote in the Plaza de España. And palaces. The Torre de los Lujanes, the Hospicio, the Liria Palace, and the Royal Palace, where we spent one whole day wandering up and down marble stairs and peering into chambers and antechambers.

We spent another day at the Prado Museum, making the proper noises in front of paintings by El Greco, Ribera, Coello, Zurbarán, Cano, Murillo, Velázquez, and Goya. I like fine paintings as well as the next guy, but by the time we finished with the Prado I would have settled for five minutes with a Marilyn Monroe calendar.

We saw a game of *pelota* in the Frontón Recoletos and a pretty unfunny play at the Comedia Theater. We discovered more restaurants, bored ourselves with one local nightclub, and spent one evening admiring the variety of drinks at El Chicote's.

In between, whenever we ran into children, we stopped

while Carrasco entertained them with magic tricks. He seemed to take some special delight in doing the golf ball routine, which baffled me. He always wanted to know my reaction when he'd finished and would laugh with pleasure no matter what I said.

Each day Ernesto gave me a complete report on Carrasco's activities when he wasn't with me, and collected his two hundred pesetas. But he had nothing unusual to report, except that at a luncheon to which Don Raimundo had invited him he had met a girl and seemed to be interested in her. My only reaction to that was that it was about time.

On the following Tuesday, when Carrasco turned down an invitation to have dinner with me, pleading another date, my only feeling was one of relief. I had been in Madrid a week. I had spent a large part of my time with him and I was no nearer to knowing where he had the diamond than I had been in the beginning. I found Carrasco interesting, but not so much so that I wanted to spend all of my time with him. I had Spanish culture running out of my ears. I had listened to so much about Don Quixote that I could say with Sancho: "All so far has been tarts and fancy cakes." I liked a little meat in my diet.

I liked the little guy when I was with him, but that first afternoon I felt like a man whose nagging wife had just gone home to her mother. I went into the patio and got slightly loaded on manzanilla.

That was Tuesday. Wednesday was the same thing. So was Thursday. He was still being friendly, but he wasn't having any part of me. I might have worried about it if it hadn't been for Ernesto and his reports.

"It's the *señorita*," he explained with a worldly wink. "All the time he sees her now. They ride in the little boats in Retiro Park. They go to look at pictures. They listen to music; not flamenco, but sad, long-faced music. They go to restaurants and sit in dark corners. If she lets him hold her hand, he puffs up like a pigeon cock. I think, Señor, that a woman pumps a man's veins full of water."

"It's usually fire water," I said dryly.

"Oh, that," he said with all the scorn of a too-wise child toward sex. *"No me tome el pelo. Senhor Carrasco, es un tonto de cuatro suelas!* That *caballero* has held her hand, but that is all. He's afraid to even go as far as her wrist."

"How do you know?" I asked.

"Señor," he said, drawing himself up, "you have asked me to tell you everything that Señor Carrasco does. So I am like his shadow. The Señor Carrasco and I are closer than my mother and father nine months before I was born."

I laughed. *"Ca!* I hope not. This girl, Ernesto, who is she? What's her name?" I was remembering that there had been a girl in Lisbon. And I didn't know a damn thing about her except that she was female.

"He calls her Señorita Rivelles."

"Spanish?"

"She must be, Señor. Only a Spanish girl could say so much with her eyes."

I relaxed a little. If it was a Spanish girl, then it probably wasn't someone who knew that he had a little blue rock, worth seven hundred thousand, kicking around somewhere.

Thursday night I had a call from John Franklin in New

York. He was beginning to worry about Great Northern's expense money. I started to give him a rundown on how I'd been spending it, starting with the menus. He interrupted with a couple of well-chosen words that would probably earn the company a complaint from the overseas operators.

On Friday Carrasco was apparently still busy with his *señorita,* so I hired a car and went to Aranjuez for the week-end.

I came back from Aranjuez on Monday morning. I went directly to my room in the hotel and put away a few things I'd taken along for the weekend. I took a shower and changed clothes. I checked with the desk. There were no phone messages or mail for me. I went downstairs, intending to walk over to the Puerto del Sol to meet Ernesto. But it was still an hour before lunchtime, so I turned into the patio. I'd have a leisurely drink and then go along.

I stopped in the entrance to the patio, looking for a table where I could look out on the street.

"Don Milo," I heard someone call. I looked around. It was Carrasco, his face beaming. Like a diamond, I thought to myself. He was waving for me to come to his table. The expression on his face, I suspected, was not so much for me but for the girl who sat with him.

She was a surprise. I hadn't thought much about it when Ernesto told me that Carrasco was interested in a girl, but I had imagined that she might be a mousy little girl with the beginnings of a mustache on her upper lip. This one was a far cry from that vague picture. Her hair was dark blond, like a perfect mixture of yellow and brown. The tips of it brushed her shoulders. Her skin was dark enough to make her blue eyes startling. The rest of her was just as eye-catching.

Maybe, I thought as I walked toward them, he wouldn't mind so much now if I got the diamond back. I couldn't imagine any man wanting to gaze at a hunk of carbon when she was around.

"Don Milo," he said as I came up, "I was looking for you over the weekend. I was sorry to hear that you had gone away, but I trust that you enjoyed yourself."

"It was all right," I said. The blonde looked even better at close range. "I left on a sudden impulse."

He glanced at the blonde and then back at me, with the expression of a small boy who has just reached the shelf with the jam. "Elena," he said to her, "this is my good friend Don Milo March, from North America. Don Milo, I would like you to meet the former Señorita Elena Rivelles."

That jarred me. I stopped what I was about to say. "Former?" I asked.

He beamed again. "I have the honor to say that she is now Señora Carrasco."

I managed not to look too surprised. *"Muchas felicidades,"* I said.

"Gracias," the blonde said. "Sansón has told me so much about you, Don Milo. I am very happy to meet you." She gave me her hand.

"Join us for a drink, Don Milo," Carrasco said.

I looked at the blonde. "Please do," she said.

I was curious. She still didn't seem like the kind of girl who would marry Carrasco; yet one look at him was enough to show that he didn't look on it as a marriage of convenience. There was something else strange about her. Part of it was the way she looked at me; there was too much curiosity in her gaze for such a new bride. There was something else that was even harder to pin down. There was no doubt that she was Spanish, yet she was different from any Spanish woman I'd ever met. There was an air about her that seemed American, or maybe Continental. It was enough to make me want to know more about her.

Carrasco beckoned the waiter and ordered a fresh bottle of wine.

"This was rather sudden, wasn't it?" I asked.

"Oh, yes," said Carrasco. For a moment I thought he was going to blush. "I met her only last week and we were married on Saturday."

"Sansón was so impetuous," the blonde murmured. She didn't sound as if she meant it, but I could see Carrasco's chest swelling.

"How did you manage it?" I wanted to know. "I thought that quick marriages weren't possible in Spain—especially for foreigners."

"It is so," he said. "You remember introducing me to Don Raimundo?"

I nodded.

"Don Raimundo graciously saw to it that I was invited to a luncheon given by his cousin, Don Esteban María Paulino y Aranda. It was there that I met Elena. When she consented to marry me, we appealed to Don Esteban. Since neither of us is Catholic, it was arranged for us to have an immediate civil ceremony."

"Enchufe?" I asked.

"Enchufe," he said happily. He'd had his first taste of influence in a country where everything was influence, and he liked it almost as much as he did what it had brought him.

"I've heard Don Raimundo mention his cousin," I said, "but I've never met him. Does he hold an important position?"

"He is very close to El Caudillo," Carrasco said mysteriously. I suspected that he was being mysterious because he didn't know how close the relationship was. I turned to look at the blonde.

"Are you also of Don Estebán's family, Señora?" I asked.

"No, Don Milo. Don Estebán was a friend of my father's. That is how I happened to be at the luncheon. My father was also a friend of El Caudillo—but he died during the war."

"I'm sorry, Señora," I said.

There was no doubting Carrasco's happiness. He was as filled with amazement that this woman had married him as I was. But he couldn't contain his happiness. He slapped me suddenly on the shoulder.

"Enough of Don this and Señora that," he said. "In—in your North American country, when people are friends, do they not call each other straight out by their first names?"

I nodded.

"Then this is the way it shall be with the three of us. You are my very good friend, my only friend, and you shall be Elena's as well. What about that, Elena?"

"It shall be as you say, Sansón," the blonde answered. She smiled at me. There was a mixture of reserve and invitation in her smile.

For just a minute I felt a pang of sorrow for the little man with us. He was in his early forties. For the first time in his life he had found a woman who he thought loved him and a man he thought was his friend. He was probably wrong on both counts. He was certainly wrong on the second count. I think at that moment I would have liked to have been his friend—but there were two corpses and sixty-seven carats between us. There was no room even for sorrow, and I pushed it away from me. I wasn't sure it would stay away.

The waiter came with the wine and filled the three glasses. I lifted mine first.

"Salud y pesetas y amor," I said.

"Salud," they both said and we drank.

"Perhaps I should have said it differently," I said, lifting my glass again. *"Salud y diamantes"*—I wished I could have watched them both at once, but he was the dangerous one; something stirred deep in his eyes at the mention of diamonds, then subsided as I reached out and touched the diamond on her finger; and I finished the toast—*"y amor y niños."* I looked at her. I couldn't be sure, but I thought there was a new interest in her gaze.

At the mention of children Carrasco blushed. *"Niños,"* he repeated. "You shouldn't have said that, Milo."

He sounded so shocked, the blonde and I both laughed. Reddening still more, he joined us.

"I wish," he said, "we could all have dinner together tonight, but Elena and I are going house-hunting and we shall probably not come back until late. Will you have dinner with us tomorrow night, Milo?"

"Please do," she said before I could answer.

I nodded. "Where are you going to look for a house?"

"Alcalá de Henares," he said.

"Darling," the blonde said firmly, "I think we should look in Guadalajara."

"You see," he said to me with a little smile, "already I am being bossed. What do you think I should do, Milo?"

"El consejo de la mujer es poco, y él que no le toma es loco," I said. I was quoting from *Don Quixote* and I was sure he'd recognize it. "A woman's advice is of little worth and he who won't take it is a fool."

He nodded in delighted recognition. The blonde laughed, but her heart wasn't in it.

"Sansón Carrasco is Bachelor no more," I added.

Elena looked her question. He explained about the Bachelor Sansón Carrasco in *Don Quixote.* "But my namesake's Bachelorhood," he continued, "came from the university rather than his own restraint."

"University poses, Elena disposes," she said, and he beamed at her.

They left shortly after that, promising that we'd meet on the following evening. I watched them go, noticing the proud way he escorted her past the other tables. The eyes of every man in the patio followed the delicate motion of her hips, and he had an instinctual awareness of it and seemed to grow in stature as he neared the door.

Some of my pity returned. I knew he was a criminal and I was well aware that he was sick, but I knew something else, too. Here was a man who had deprived himself of everything until he was past forty; then suddenly it was all showered on him in less than a week—money, a rare diamond (somewhere!), influential friends, and a desirable woman. I think for a minute I envied him and felt a sadness for the loss that would have to be his.

Then I suddenly thought of Ernesto. I left the patio quickly; I was in time. Carrasco and the blonde were already in their rented car, but it had not yet pulled away from the curb. Ernesto was standing nearby, neatly dividing his gaze between the vigilant doorman and the rear of the car. I caught his attention in time and shook my head. I didn't want Ernesto trying to ride a rear bumper for the more than fifty miles to Guadalajara.

He strolled down the Carrera de San Jerónimo and I walked after him. When we were a couple of blocks from the hotel, he lingered to let me catch up.

I paid him for the days I'd been away and assured him he'd get paid for this day even though he didn't have to work. His report didn't give me anything. He had plenty of details, but nothing pointed to what I wanted.

That afternoon I once more picked the lock on Carrasco's door and took a prolonged look through his room. It was wasted time. He still had a few small diamonds wrapped up and tucked away in a drawer, but there was no sign of the big one. Everything was about the same as on my first visit, except for his golf balls and thimbles resting in one drawer, and the things belonging to the blonde. By the time I was finished, I was convinced that there was no place where anything could be hidden in that room.

I went through the blonde's things, too, hoping that I might find out something more about her. But all I learned was what perfume she liked. It was a kind meant to turn better heads than Carrasco's.

Then I got what I thought was a bright idea. I went back to the drawer with the golf balls. I'd seen him do the trick of the vanishing balls and I knew it was done with a shell; if there could be a hollow half-ball, why not a whole one? It made sense. It fit with the way Carrasco thought. I kicked myself for not coming up with the idea before and grabbed the golf balls.

So much for my bright ideas. I went over every one of those balls like a wino looking for the last drop in a bottle. No seams. But I knew that a good craftsman, working with a jeweler's lathe, could do wonders. I wasted another half hour trying to unscrew the two halves of each ball. It was like the old gag of unscrewing the inscrutable. I was working on the last one when I caught sight of myself in the mirror—hunched over that damned golf ball like a squirrel trying to crack a nut.

I grinned at myself and gave up. I went over to the Avenida de José Antonio and went to a movie. A Spanish movie starring Luchy Soto. Except for her, it was strictly Grade B.

That night I had dinner alone in Chicote's and then went to bed early.

The next morning I saw Carrasco for a moment in the lobby. I asked him about the house and he said they hadn't found anything they liked in Guadalajara. When I grinned, he said that Elena had promised they would look in Alcalá de Henares. He reminded me that we were having dinner together that night and told me to meet them at La Sevillana. Then he left to take cigarettes to Elena.

It was a little before ten that night when I went to La Sevillana. There was a group of children not far from the entrance, all of them begging. Among them was Ernesto; I knew Carrasco and the blonde were already there. I distributed a handful of céntimos and went in.

They were at a table in the corner. In front of them was a bottle of manzanilla and a plate filled with salted almonds, olives, *jamón serrano* or raw ham, and anchovies in oil. He was talking with great animation. She was listening, but she looked bored. As I drew closer I could hear he was telling her the sort of house he wanted to find. He had it complete down to the last nail. He'd probably spent twenty years building it in his mind.

"Hola," I said, stopping by the table. I looked down at them.

"Milo," he exclaimed with obvious pleasure. He jumped to his feet and eagerly clasped my hand. His warmth was so genuine that again I had to force the future out of my mind.

I looked down at the blonde. She was wearing a black dress, cut low but finished off with lace so that there were brief glimpses of the tops of her breasts. I gave up the unequal contest with the lace and looked at her face. Her eyes were laughing at me.

"Siéntese usted en esta silla, Milo," she said, patting the chair next to her. "We should have waited for you, but we weren't sure how soon you'd be here."

I pulled out the chair and sat down. "No reason why you should have waited," I said. I turned to him. "I saw the usual bunch of kids outside. I suppose you entertained them as always."

"No," he said. He looked embarrassed. "Elena asked me not to, so I've been leaving the magic in our room."

"I don't mind the magic," she said, smiling. "Sansón is really very clever. But I do object to standing on the street while he entertains beggars."

"She's right," he said amiably. He poured manzanilla into my glass and lifted his own. *"Salud y pesetas,"* he said.

"Y amor," the blonde added. She was looking at me over the edge of her glass.

"Y niños," I said.

"Todavía no," she said. *"No corre prisa."*

"No hay tiempo que perder," I said. "There's no time to waste."

Carrasco was blushing. *"No me tome el pelo,"* he said. "Don't make fun of me."

"No more, *amigo,*" I said. *"Salud y dicha."*

We drank to health and happiness, and Carrasco began telling me about the houses they had seen the day before.

After a while we ordered our dinner. We all had *cocido,* which is chicken, chickpeas, potatoes, greens, sausage, bacon, and saffron, all cooked together like a boiled dinner. But to call it a boiled dinner is like calling a Cadillac a car.

We finished dinner and ordered dessert. When the waiter left, Carrasco excused himself and went to the men's room. There was a sudden silence with his going. I looked at the blonde and found her staring at me, her gaze filled with speculation. She picked up her half-filled wine glass.

"A toast?" she asked.

"Sure," I said. "Why not?"

"Salud y diamantes," she said.

"Health and diamonds? I'll drink to that." I lifted my glass and drained it. "Too bad there isn't a fireplace in which we can break our glasses."

She put her glass back on the table without touching it to her lips. She leaned forward so that it was difficult for me to keep from playing peekaboo with that lace dress again.

"Who are you?" she asked.

"Milo March."

"Something like a geologist?" she asked scornfully.

"Something like that," I said easily.

"Why are you so friendly with my husband?" she asked.

"Why not?" I returned. "I find him to be a most interesting man."

"A otro perro con ese hueso," she said. Her voice reminded me of Ernesto's when he had also told me to "give that bone to another dog."

I tried to look surprised. Well-born Spanish ladies didn't talk like that. But the subtlety of my expression escaped her.

"My husband arrived in Madrid from Lisbon on a Sunday. Two days later you also arrived from Lisbon." I wondered how she'd discovered that. I'd given Carrasco the idea that I came by way of Paris. It looked like someone else had been enriching the customs officials. "You went to the same hotel where my husband was staying and immediately made friends with him."

"We became friendly when I caught a thief entering your

husband's room," I said. "Or do you think I arranged that, too?"

"Perhaps," she said. "What is it you want?"

I grinned at her. *"Salud y pesetas y amor,"* I said.

"What about diamonds?" she asked.

"I have nothing against diamonds. I wouldn't want to run barefoot through a roomful of diamonds, but I like them."

"What about big blue diamonds?"

"Why should a diamond be blue?" I asked. "It has everything in life to look forward to—including the desire of beautiful women."

Carrasco was coming across the restaurant toward the table.

"Whatever you're planning," she said swiftly, "I suggest that you forget it and stay away from my husband. It may not give you the money or love, but that way you can be sure of your health."

"Querida," I said. "I didn't know you cared. How can I stay away now that you're interested?"

Her expression indicated that she had some ideas along that line, too, but Carrasco was already at the table and she confined it to looking.

"Well," said Carrasco, "what were you two so deep in conversation about?"

"You," I told him. "We were remarking how each of us is so attached to you, Sansón. In different ways, of course."

"Sansón knows how much I love him," the blonde said. Her voice had just the right softness, but her eyes were cold.

He reached over and patted her hand. "And Milo is a good friend," he said. "It is not often that a man is so fortunate as to have a loving wife, a good friend, and—" He was staring off into space, seemingly unaware that he'd broken off.

I realized that the blonde and I were both tense, hanging on the edge of that broken sentence. I deliberately broke the spell by leaning back and laughing.

"Don't forget Don Quixote," I said.

His eyes came back into focus and he smiled. "And Don Quixote, of course," he said.

The waiter arrived with our *tartas,* coffee, and *aguardiente* brandy. The conversation lost its undertones as Carrasco started talking about Don Quixote.

When we got back to the hotel, I said good night and went to my room. I put in a call to John Franklin in New York. It was too late for the office to be open, but the operator found him at home.

"What's up?" he asked as soon as he heard my voice.

"Nothing you want to hear," I said. "I'm no closer to the sparkler than I was before. But I want to know something. Did you ever hear of a girl named Elena Rivelles? A beautiful blonde. And stacked."

He was silent a minute. "I don't remember the name," he said finally. "Should I?"

"I don't know," I said truthfully, "All I know is that she's after the same thing. Maybe she's an amateur, but I wouldn't bet on it."

"I'll try to check up on her and call you back tomorrow," he said. "Anything else?"

"Nothing," I said and hung up. I had a last cigarette and went to sleep.

The next day was Wednesday. I'd been in Madrid a week and I wasn't any nearer to the Tavernier Blue than I had been the first day.

Downstairs, I asked about the Carrascos. I was told that Señor Carrasco had left in a rented car and that Señora Carrasco was upstairs, indisposed. I was going to phone her, but the operator told me that she had left word that she didn't want to take any calls.

I went over to the Puerto del Sol and found Ernesto.

"The Señor Carrasco went to Alcalá de Henares," he said. "I did not follow him because you said it was not necessary."

"Visto bueno," I told him. I handed him his money.

"What is it with this one, Señor?" he asked me. "Why is it we are watching him? Perhaps he's a spy."

"You've been listening to Radio Nacional," I told him, naming the Falangist network. "The Señor took something which did not belong to him and killed two people while he was doing it."

"That one?" he asked in scorn.

"That one," I said. "Don't be fooled by the way he looks, Ernesto. He's a bad *hombre* when he wants to be."

"And you, Señor?" he asked. "You will steal this thing away from him when you learn where it is?"

I laughed. "No, Ernesto." I looked at him. "You are truly my partner, Ernesto?"

"Truly, Señor."

"Señor Carrasco is wanted by the police in North America. When I learn where he has the stolen object, he will be turned over to the police."

"Why not just grab him and beat it out of him, Señor?"

"No, Ernesto. It is perhaps one form of justice, but not for my stomach."

"Truly, Señor?"

"Truly, Ernesto."

"You are of the police, Señor?"

"Not quite, Ernesto," I said. "Sometimes I work with them. Sometimes they seem to think I'm working against them."

His eyes brightened. "Just like Don Humfrio?" he said eagerly.

"Don Humfrio?" I asked.

"The celebrated American detective," he explained patiently. "Don Humfrio Bogart."

"There are a few differences," I said dryly. "I don't have a trenchcoat."

"Qué es eso?"

"Never mind," I told him. "It's a local joke and it should have stayed there."

"What is this valuable object, Señor?"

"We'll skip that, too," I said. "We are truly partners, but this might be too much temptation for you."

He shrugged.

"I'll see you tomorrow, Ernesto," I said.

"Hasta mañana," he said cheerfully.

I had lunch and then went back to the hotel. I was just in time to see Elena Carrasco leaving. She looked as if "indisposed" was a polite term for raging mad.

I picked up a paperback mystery novel—*Ninguna Tumba*

para Marzo*—and went up to my room. I read until long after the siesta period was over. Then I fell asleep.

The cocktail hour was in full swing when I came down. I looked in the American Bar. Sansón and Elena were at the bar. He waved and I went over. I mentioned that I'd heard Elena hadn't felt well that morning and that I hoped she had recovered.

She said she was feeling fine, but her mind seemed to be on something else.

"Can you imagine," Carrasco said, "she wasn't feeling well, but she wouldn't let me stay to take care of her. She insisted that I go off to Alcalá de Henares and look at houses."

"It wasn't anything serious, darling," she said. "It was only a headache and it was gone by lunch."

"That reminds me," he said. He shook a finger playfully at me. "My friend, you have fallen down on your self-appointed task. You have failed as my guardian angel."

"In what way?" I asked.

"This afternoon, after Elena went out, someone broke into our room. You weren't there to capture the thief."

"Sorry," I said. "What was taken?"

"Nothing. But our things were thrown all over the room. The manager thinks perhaps it was not a real thief. He says there is a lot of anti-foreigner feeling in Madrid and it may be the result of that."

"Against Argentina?" I asked.

"Who knows?" he said, shrugging.

---

* The Spanish title of *No Grave for March*, the second Milo March mystery—another private joke?

I had a hunch. I looked at Elena. She was staring innocently into her drink. Too innocently. I remembered the way she'd looked when I saw her leaving the hotel.

Carrasco wanted me to have dinner with them again, but I made vague noises about having another date. I didn't feel up to watching the poor guy in the middle while the two of us waited for him to make a slip.

I went off to dinner by myself. To a restaurant called Botín, where they served roasted suckling pig. But even that didn't cheer me up.

I was feeling depressed about the whole thing. Not only because I wasn't making any headway. I'd been trying to keep the larger picture out of my mind, but it wasn't working too well. Sansón Carrasco—or Samson Carter, it didn't make much difference which—was a nice little guy. I liked him. Murderer, yes—but that was his sickness. In a way it was a sickness of the past. If everything had been as uncomplicated afterward as he so naively assumed, he'd probably never commit another crime. If …

But pretty soon he was going to find out that the guy he'd come to think was his friend—his first and only friend—was just a watchdog for the insurance company. And pretty soon he was going to find out that the woman he thought loved him was just another broad with an itch for a big diamond. I knew it was going to be more than he could take, and I didn't want to have to watch it.

I made up my mind about one thing. If I didn't find the diamond within the next couple of days, I was going to see that the American cops got him, diamond or no diamond.

Maybe that would still leave him the illusion of Elena to cling to.

After dinner I went back to the hotel. There was a message that the overseas operator had been trying to reach me. I tried to call John Franklin. The office was closed and he wasn't at home. I said to hell with it and went to bed.

I'd been in bed maybe an hour, but I was still awake, when I heard a noise at my door. Someone was gently turning the knob. I remained quiet and listened. In a minute I heard the door open and someone came into my room. The door closed softly and then there was silence. I waited.

The moon was shining in through one window in my room, throwing a silver patch of light a few feet square. There was the sound of movement in the room and someone stepped directly into the moonlight. It was Elena Carrasco.

She was wearing a dark robe that reached to the floor. The moonlight on her hair made it seem lighter than it was. She turned until she stood in profile. She lifted her hands to her throat. There was the singing of a zipper and the robe dropped to the floor. She wore nothing beneath it.

For a minute I forgot who she was—forgot everything except that she was a beautiful woman. She was silhouetted against the moonlight. The firm curve of her breasts, the almost imperceptible swell of her stomach, the long sweeping lines of her legs were outlined in silver and I could feel my breath quicken.

"You approve?" she asked softly. She spoke in English as perfectly as she spoke in Spanish. There was no trace of an accent.

"I approve," I said. "How did you know I was awake? Or did you count on this being a sight that would awaken any man?"

She laughed deeply in her throat so that it was almost a purr. "I knew you were awake," she said. "I could tell by your breathing once I was inside."

"Sounds like you've had a lot of experience," I said.

She laughed again and moved out of the moonlight, leaving the crumpled robe on the floor behind her. "Where are your cigarettes?" she asked.

"My coat's hanging on the back of a chair near where you are now," I said. "Cigarettes and matches in the right-hand pocket."

I could hear her fumbling with my coat and then she came toward me. As she neared me, the outlines of her body emerged from the darkness. She sat down on the edge of the bed.

"Hello, Milo," she said softly.

"Hello, Elena."

She leaned over and pressed her mouth against mine. Her lips were like soft flames. Her breasts brushed lightly against my bare chest. The warm scent of her body reached out to pull me closer.

It's a funny thing. I knew she wanted something. It wasn't just my masculine appeal that had brought her into my room. I knew also that she was the wife of a guy who would be more grievously hurt than I could possibly be rewarded by our brief mingling of flesh. I wasn't in love with her; I hadn't even been attracted to her until this moment. But none of these things mattered. Desire can wall off the rest of the world and set up its own retreat.

She straightened up, but my chest still tingled where her breasts had briefly kissed me. I reached up to pull her down beside me.

"Not yet, Milo," she said. She reached out and put a cigarette in my mouth. "I want to talk to you."

"At a time like this," I told her, "I'm not much good at small talk."

"This is big talk," she said. She struck a match and held it for me. The light flickered across her body as she lit our cigarettes. Then she blew it out and we were in darkness again. "Are you a cop, Milo?"

"I'm no cop," I said.

"I thought not." She pulled deeply on the cigarette, throwing a red light down over her breasts. "You know about the Tavernier Blue?"

"I know about it," I admitted.

"Sixty-seven carats of blue diamond," she said dreamily. "Seven hundred thousand dollars. You know what we could do with that much money, Milo?"

"What could we do?"

"Everything," she said. She sounded a little hysterical. "We could go away together. With seven hundred thousand dollars there wouldn't be anything to interfere with this—" She leaned over and kissed me again. Her lips clung to mine for a minute, then pulled reluctantly away. She'd started this in cold blood, but things were warming up. The only hitch was that she wanted the diamond even more.

"The Tavernier Blue—and me, Milo," she said.

"What's the matter, honey?" I asked. "You tore the room apart today and couldn't find anything?"

She called Carrasco a name. A good Anglo-Saxon name. "I married that little shrimp," she said, "just to get my hands on that diamond. I've gone through everything he owns. I've searched his clothes at night when he takes them off. I went through every inch of our room. Where the hell is it?" Her rage subsided. She reached out and trailed her fingers across my chest. "Do you know where it is, Milo?"

"No," I said.

"But we could find it together," she said. "If you'll help me, Milo, we'll get the Tavernier Blue. Will you?"

I was curious. I reached up and touched her breasts. A tremor ran through her body.

"If I do," I said gently, "you'll stay here?"

"Yes," she said eagerly. "I'll have to go back before the night is over, but until then …"

"And if I don't?"

I could feel the struggle within her, but there was no doubt what would win. The diamond would.

She pulled away from my hand. "You want the diamond for yourself," she said flatly. "You'll never get it."

It works both ways. A few minutes earlier, if I'd had the diamond under my pillow I probably wouldn't have cared if she took it. But she had talked too much. What she had to offer was all wrapped up in strings. There are some things I don't like to bargain for, and this was one of them. She had tried to talk me into something; she had succeeded in talking me out of it.

"I'll bet," I said, "you're so hard you'd cut glass yourself. Run along to Sansón, honey. I don't think I want you—with or without."

She left the bed without a word. She appeared in the moonlight and scooped up the robe, flinging it around her. She was still a beautiful woman, but it didn't mean a thing.

I heard her open the door, then she spoke. "You'll get neither, Señor March," she said softly. She had switched back to Spanish. "But you'll remember me, *chico.*"

The door closed softly but with the intensity of a slam.

She had taken my cigarettes with her. I got up and took another package from the dresser drawer. I lit one and stretched out on the bed.

The telephone rang. I reached out and lifted the receiver. It was the overseas operator. A moment later I heard John Franklin's voice.

"Where were you earlier?" he asked.

"Dinner," I said. "Having roasted suckling pig."

He groaned. "On the stockholder's money," he said. "Don't itemize that on your expense account or they'll have me served on a tray. With an apple in my mouth."

"A tasty thought," I said. "You got something for me?"

"Yeah. Remember this Elena Rivelles you asked about?"

"Sure," I said, remembering the way she'd looked in the moonlight. "She's got a record?"

"She's got one. Elena Rivelles, by the way, is her real name. She was born in Spain. Twenty-five years ago. Her father was an army officer who was killed in the civil war. She was adopted by another officer who was on Franco's staff. She left

Spain when she was sixteen. Since then she's been arrested in six countries, including here, but nobody kept her long. She's a smart cookie."

"What kind of charges?" I asked.

"The first one was for soliciting in London," he said. "The rest of them have all been jewelry jobs. At the moment she's wanted for questioning in Paris. Is she there?"

"She's here," I said, not bothering to add how near she was—or how near she'd almost been.

"She doesn't usually work alone. She's been known to work with four or five of the top men, including Martin Lomer. The Paris job she's wanted on is the same one that pulled in Rainer Eckholdt."

"What the hell is this?" I said. "A convention of the Ancient Order of Diamond Admirers?"

"Can you blame them, Milo?" he asked. "The Tavernier Blue. Seven hundred thousand bucks. That's why you've got to beat them to it."

"I'll beat them to it," I said, "but don't ask me how. What are the New York cops doing?"

"Homicide is sending a man. Maybe they've already sent him. I threw around as much weight as I could and I think he'll look you up before he does anything, but don't expect any more than that. I don't think he'll give you any cooperation."

"I never expect any from a cop," I said. "Anything else?"

"Only that the Board of Directors are getting a little nervous."

"Tell them to relax with the *Wall Street Journal,*" I said. "Good night." I hung up.

I put out my cigarette and stretched out again. I tried relaxing by thinking what it might have been like if the night had turned out differently.

I was just starting to drift off to sleep when there was a knock on my door. Annoyed, I dragged myself back. My room was becoming as popular as the Estación del Norte.

"Who's there?" I asked.

"Guardia," said a muffled voice through the door.

That jarred me all the way awake. I couldn't imagine what the police wanted. I got out of bed and switched on the light. I found my bathrobe and slipped it on. Then I opened the door.

There were two of them, looking very neat in their uniforms. They were also looking grim.

"Your name, Señor?" one of them asked.

"Milo March," I said.

They looked at each other and nodded. "Your passport, please," the one asked.

I didn't get it. The only thing I could think of at the moment was that somebody had seen Elena coming into my room or leaving it. But that was hardly a matter for two cops.

"Come in," I said. They stepped into the room and I closed the door. I went over to my coat, hanging on the back of a chair, and reached into the inside pocket. Then I got the shock of my life. My passport and residence visa were both gone.

For a minute I was paralyzed, trying to think what had happened. Then I remembered Elena asking for cigarettes. I told her they were in my coat. I'd heard her fumbling with the coat.

"Cómo?" the policeman said.

"I'm afraid that my passport's been stolen," I said, "but if you'll get in touch with the American Embassy, it will be straightened out. Or, for that matter, with your own Dirección General de Seguridad. They gave me a residence visa, which has also been stolen."

The two officers exchanged glances again.

"You'd better get dressed, Señor. You are under arrest."

"Look," I said, "why can't we use the phone and settle this right now? It's silly to arrest me because somebody's stolen my passport."

"Sorry, Señor," the same one said. "We were told that you would try to claim that your passport was stolen."

"Well, it was. I can even point out the person who stole it."

He shrugged. "Señor," he said patiently, "it has been pointed out to us that you are one who has entered the country illegally. If this is not true, I am sure you can straighten it out, but in the meantime you must get dressed and come with us."

"Where?" I asked.

"The Dirección General de Seguridad in the Puerto del Sol," he said.

There was no point in arguing. Maybe when we got there I could get somebody to look up the records of residence visas issued. I got into my clothes.

"Can I at least phone someone?" I asked when I was dressed.

"Later, Señor," he said. "Come on."

Cops, I thought. They're the same no matter what country you're in. I felt like taking a swing at this one, but I knew it would be a mistake. To an American a Spanish cop may look like somebody out of a comic opera, but they can shoot just as straight as the American ones. I walked ahead of them into the corridor.

It seemed to me that the doorway to Room 619 was partly open and somebody was peering out, but I may have imagined it.

NINE

The streets of Madrid are still very much alive after midnight. When we arrived in Puerto del Sol, the cafés were crowded and the street was busy with the *limpiabotas* looking for shoes to shine. Right near the entrance to police headquarters there was an old woman still selling *churros,* stringlike Spanish doughnuts, threading them on blades of strong grass. I looked for Ernesto, but he was nowhere in sight.

The two policemen led me into the building. We tramped down various corridors and finally wound up in an office. They ushered me through the door so quickly I caught only part of the name on it. The part I saw was *Información e Investigación.* That didn't make me feel any better. That was also the last half of the official name of the Falange secret police.

One of them stayed with me in the anteroom while the other one went on into the inner office. About ten minutes later he came out and motioned me in. When I stepped into the office, he closed the door behind me.

There was a row of filing cabinets, a desk, and one chair. A man was sitting in the chair. He was dressed in civilian clothes, but his authority was stamped in his face when he looked up.

"Como se llama usted?" he asked.

"Milo March."

"Nationality?"

"American."

"And you have no passport?" he said.

"I do have a passport," I said. "Also a residence visa. But they were both stolen sometime tonight just before the two officers came to my room. I explained that to them."

"Oh, yes," he said. "Is it not interesting, Señor, that a citizen of Spain has reported you as a foreigner in this country illegally and that when the officers arrive to ask you about this, your passport has just that moment been stolen?"

"Interesting but not so strange," I said. "The citizen of Spain who reported me is undoubtedly the same citizen of Spain who took my passport. I find it more interesting that this citizen, Elena Rivelles de Carrasco, is an international criminal. At the moment she is wanted by the police of Paris."

He shuffled the papers on his desk—the gesture of international officialdom.

"It is usual for those brought in here to start accusing those they think have informed on them," he said.

"Ya basta!" I snapped. "All you have to do is check right here in this building where I was given my residence visa."

"That office is closed, Señor."

"Then check with the American Embassy."

"The Embassy is also closed, Señor. All of those things will be checked tomorrow, of course."

"And in the meantime?"

"You are under arrest. It is a very serious charge, Señor, and we must hold you."

"I have a right to see my Ambassador," I said. "Whatever

I'm charged with, you have to let me get in touch with him. I demand that he be called now."

"*Ahora, ahora,*" he said. That was like saying "Right away" but not meaning it. "Why are you in Spain, Señor March?"

"Vacation," I said shortly.

"Oh? Do you always go on vacations without a passport?"

"I told you I had a passport and residence visa, and they were stolen."

"Oh, yes, so you did," he said pleasantly. He shuffled the papers on his desk again. That soft rustling, I thought, was the theme music of the concentration camps of Europe. "Are you working for Russia, Señor March?"

For a minute I was startled. I wondered if this was more of Elena's work, but then I realized that it was probably a normal conclusion for a Fascist. The minute something was not in order, the Fascist smelled Communism and the Communist smelled fascism.

"No," I said.

"Are you a Communist, Señor?"

"No."

"Why did you come to Spain?"

"Vacation," I repeated.

"*Es un cuento absurdo,*" he snapped. He aimed an index finger at me. "Señor March, what would you say if I told you that we know that you came here to plot against Generalissimo Franco?"

"*No diga tonterías,*" I said. "Don't talk such utter foolishness. I came here on a vacation. I have a passport and a residence visa. I demand that I be permitted to call the American

Ambassador. Until then, I refuse to answer any more questions."

He stared at me, his face expressionless. "There are ways, Señor March."

"Sure," I said. "I'll bet you know all of them, too, *chico*. But I've got news for you. There are ways of making men talk and there are some men who won't talk. I'm one of them."

He looked at me a long time. Then he shrugged. "Empty your pockets," he said.

I turned out my pockets, putting everything on his desk. He picked up my package of cigarettes and matches and handed them to me. He wrote down a list of everything else, including the amount of money, and signed it with a flourish. He held it out. "Your receipt, Señor."

I took it and put it in my pocket. "Now may I call the Ambassador?" I asked.

"Ahora, ahora," he said. He raised his voice and shouted. "Tomás!"

The door opened and a policeman looked in.

"Tiene mucho pico," the man behind the desk said. "Put him away."

"Vámonos," the policeman said, jerking his head toward the door.

"What am I charged with?" I asked the man behind the desk.

"No charge," he said flatly. "You're being held for questioning."

I turned and followed the policeman out of the office. We tramped through several more corridors and finally went through a section leading to the prison.

The cop turned me over to the warder with a brief explanation of why I was there. Then he left.

The warder picked up his keys and looked at me. He was an old man, with a heavy, wrinkled face. The left sleeve of his jacket was empty. He seemed to guess what I was thinking for he shook his head at me. "The last gate you came through doesn't open from this side without the aid of a guard," he said. "Come on, Señor."

I followed him. There were four corridors radiating out from his office. We went down one of these. On each side there were two tiers of long, monotonous rows of cell doors. Each door bore a number and a spy hole, but those were the only things to break the monotony of solid steel and concrete.

Halfway down, he stopped and unlocked a door. He motioned me in and stepped in after me.

The cell was perhaps seven or eight feet long and about five feet wide. There was a toilet and a wash basin. Against one wall was a small iron table and chair that could be folded up against the wall. On the other side there was the iron bed, which could also be folded against the wall. One tiny window with iron bars and, on the outside, a fine wire netting.

The warder walked to the bed and bent over it. There was a linen tab on the edge of the straw mattress. He looked at it and grunted. He poked the mattress with a blunt figure and grunted again. He started for the door.

"Señor," I said, "I want to call the American Ambassador, or at least have him told that I am here. I am willing to pay many pesetas if you will arrange this."

He looked at me with an old shrewdness in his eyes. "You have the pesetas with you?" he asked.

"No," I said, "but I will give them to you as soon as I am released. Five thousand pesetas."

He shrugged. "Señor," he said humorlessly, "neither you nor pesetas have wings. *Buenas noches.*" He went out and locked the door.

The first few minutes in a prison cell are unique. This was not the first time I'd been in one, but I suspect no one ever becomes accustomed to it. Each re-experience has the same impact.

At first there is a kind of refusal to accept the reality. I went to the door and tried to look out through the spy hole. There was nothing to see. I went over and tried the faucets. Only one of them worked. That was better than I expected. I tried pulling the chain on the toilet. It worked, too, but it made a noise that sounded as though the pipes would burst any moment.

I walked over to the window. It was just a little higher than my head. I grabbed the bars and pulled myself up. It was too dark to see much, but it looked as if the window opened on a side street or a courtyard.

Hope flared. If it did face on the street, all I had to do was write a note addressed to the Ambassador and drop it out of the window. I started composing the note in my mind before I realized that I didn't have paper or pencil and there was probably no way I could get it. It is always this sort of thing that makes prison more real than the slamming of the steel and concrete door.

I went over and sat down on the bed. The straw mattress was so thin I could feel the steel springs through it.

I stood up and started examining the walls. They were heavily whitewashed. I tried pounding on the wall, hoping to get an answer from the neighboring cell. But there was no answer. I guessed that the sound probably didn't carry through the thick stone. And there were no exposed pipes to pound on.

There were a few names and dates scratched into the paint where previous occupants had recorded their visits. Then I noticed that beneath the paint there were other letters scratched into the rock. They were old, covered with many coats of paint, so that in some cases I had to trace the letters with my fingers to make them out. Some of them were probably the initials of prisoners, but many were the symbols of old political parties. They must have been there almost twenty years. C.N.T. and F.A.I., the initials of the Anarchist parties. On one wall I could make out a hammer and sickle. In several places I found U.G.T., the initials of the Spanish Socialist Trade Union outfit.

I tried to think about the endless line of men who had marched through this cell, most of them on their way to death, but it didn't make me feel any better. I knew enough about Franco's brand of officials to know that they could just forget about me for days—or weeks. And in the meantime Elena would be after the diamond.

I stretched out on the bed, using my arms to shield my eyes from the glare of the naked electric bulb in the ceiling. After a while I fell asleep.

It was daylight when I awakened. It took me a couple of minutes to orient myself, to realize where I was. But even before the sight of the cell impressed itself on me, the silence and the smells brought the awareness of prison. There's nothing else like the bleak quiet of a prison, where even the sounds seem locked up.

A guard soon brought breakfast—gray, tasteless oatmeal with perhaps a spoonful of weak milk over it. There was also coffee, just as tasteless as the cereal.

I renewed my demands to see the American Ambassador and got the same answer.

"*Ahora, ahora,*" said the warder.

By noon I had used the last of my cigarettes. When the warder arrived with lunch—a fish and vegetable soup drowned in garlic—I asked him about cigarettes.

"They can be purchased in the canteen," he said. "American cigarettes for fifteen pesetas."

"My money's in the office," I said. "Bring me some cigarettes and tell them to take out the amount."

He shook his head. "It is not permitted, Señor. You must pay cash for the things purchased from the canteen."

"Then get me my money," I said in ill temper. "You've no right to take it."

"*Claro que sí,*" he said with a mock bow. "The *caballero* has but to ask." He went out and the heavy door slammed shut.

The lack of cigarettes became the worst thing. I found a couple of butts on the floor, but they were short and only made the need greater. That evening the warder took enough pity on me to give me one cigarette, emphasizing that it was only a loan. I smoked half of it and saved the other half for the next morning.

The next three days dragged by in the same fashion. Three

times a day my cell door was opened and what passed for food was ladled out to me. Once a day a guard came by and watched while I cleaned out the cell. I managed to cadge two more cigarettes during that time. All of my demands were met with the same good-natured indifference.

The mealtime visits were the only outward symbol that I existed at all. Any kind of questioning would have been preferable. As it was, I began to feel that I was just going to be left in that cell and no one would know where I was. A dozen times a day I figured out ways to get a message out, only to abandon each one as I realized it was impractical.

It was midmorning on the fourth day when I heard the door being unlocked. It was not the usual time and I sprang up from the bed in excitement.

It was the warder. "Come with me, Señor," he said.

"I'm freed?" I asked.

"No se afane tanto," he said. "You are being permitted a visitor. That is all."

"A visitor?" I exclaimed. My thoughts whirled. I could think of no one who would be visiting me, but it was unimportant. The fact that someone knew where I was meant everything. I lost my feeling of being isolated and became almost gay as we walked down the corridor.

"Your nephew," the warder said. "The visit would not have been permitted if the boy had also been a foreigner. Señor, you should have told us that you had family in Spain."

At the moment I couldn't think of any nephews, but I wasn't going to ask questions. I was so glad to get out of that cell that I would have gone to visit with Franco himself.

He led me into a large room. In the center of it was a sort of iron cage, round in shape and large enough to hold thirty or thirty-five persons. The warder unlocked a door in the cage and motioned me inside.

"You're allowed ten minutes," he said as he locked the door. He turned and left.

The door opened and Ernesto came in. The minute I saw him I realized that it couldn't have been anyone else. I should have guessed the minute I heard that my "nephew" was the visitor.

"*Hola, tío,*" he said as he reached the cage. "Hello, uncle."

"I," I said solemnly, "never thought I'd live to see the day when I'd be glad to claim you as a relative, but this is it. How did you find out I was here?"

"It was nothing, Señor," he said, shrugging his thin shoulders. "When you had not shown up by late yesterday, I thought perhaps you had run out on the six hundred pesetas you owed me—you will forgive me, Señor, but such things do happen. My mother's cousin works in the kitchen at the Palace, so I went to see if he could tell me anything. He was able to learn that you were seen in the company of *agentes de policía* three nights before and have not been seen since. From Rosa, the old one who sells *churros,* I learned that you were brought in here. Then the brother of Jorge, who sells hand soap on the Calle de Alcalá, is a guard in here, and he was able to determine that you were being held. That was all, Señor."

"Did you have any trouble getting in?" I asked.

"*Ca!* It was easy, Señor. I merely said you were my uncle

and that my mother was in tears to know that you were still alive. All I had to do was think of my six hundred pesetas and my own tears flowed as water."

"You'll have to wait until I get out for your pesetas," I said. I quickly told him all that had happened. "Now, Ernesto," I continued, "you must do one thing for me. Go to the American Embassy and tell the Ambassador that I am here. Then it shouldn't take long."

"At once, Señor. My pesetas will lend wings to my feet."

"Now, if you only had some cigarettes, I would love you like a—a nephew."

"Ahora mismo," he said with a grin. His hand dived into his ragged clothes and came out with a package of cheap Spanish cigarettes. But they were cigarettes. And a full package. He handed them through the bars. "That will be an extra five pesetas—when you get your money," he said.

"Gladly," I said. "I didn't know you smoked or I would have asked before this." I started to open the pack.

"I don't. Those came from the pocket of the warder." He must have misunderstood my look of surprise. "It was all he had in his pockets, Señor," he added apologetically.

I decided I'd better wait for the privacy of my cell to smoke. I put the cigarettes in my pocket. Just in time, too, for the warder came back at that moment to announce that the visit was over.

"Hasta mañana, tío," Ernesto said. He dodged around the warder and was gone.

The warder unlocked the cage and we started back through the corridors.

"Your nephew returns tomorrow?" he asked.

"If it is permitted," I said.

"I see no reason why not. He will bring you cigarettes, even some money?"

"I imagine so," I said. I knew the sudden civility came from the possibility of tips for small favors if I got some money.

"Your nephew seems a bright boy," he observed.

"The brightest," I said, glad he couldn't know how bright.

He unlocked the door of my cell and then followed me inside.

"Since you will be getting some tomorrow," he said, "perhaps I might advance you a cigarette or two." He reached into his pocket and a look of surprise came over his face. He hurriedly investigated his other pockets. "Strange," he muttered. "I had a package of cigarettes …"

"Perhaps you dropped them somewhere," I suggested, restraining my smile.

"It is to be hoped not," he said. He was still exploring the same pockets. "To drop things around here is not safe. No one will admit to finding anything."

I reached in my pockets and managed to extract two cigarettes from the package. I brought them out. "My nephew gave me two cigarettes today," I said. "Do me the honor of taking one of them."

"*Gracias,*" he said. He took one of the cigarettes. He looked at it and seemed disappointed that it wasn't an American cigarette. But he put it in his mouth and struck a match, holding it for me. "Strange … ," he said again. He went back to slapping at his empty pockets as he walked out of the cell.

When the door had closed behind him, I sank down on the bed and collapsed with laughter. It was the first time I had laughed in almost four days, and it made me a little drunk. Or maybe it was the cigarette.

The next day at about the same time the warder returned to announce that my nephew was once more there. That morning I had been increasingly nervous. I had imagined all sorts of things: that they wouldn't let Ernesto in again, that he wouldn't even try to see the Ambassador. ... But my good humor returned with the warder.

We went back to that same room and the warder once more locked me in the cage. He left and Ernesto came in.

"You saw the Ambassador?" I asked before he was even near the cage.

He shook his head and my heart sank.

"I tried, Señor," he said quickly, "but it is not easy. You and I know that I am truly your partner, but to others I am merely a *limpiabotas*. They would not let me inside the door. But do not worry, Señor, I have set machinery in motion."

"What kind of machinery?" I asked dubiously.

"I have mentioned the matter to my mother's cousin in the kitchen of the Palace. He will speak of it to an assistant chef, who will tell it to the chef. He in turn will have a word with the assistant manager, who will speak to the manager, and then the manager will telephone your Ambassador."

It sounded highly unworkable to me and I said as much. "You will see, Señor," he said. "Once it is pointed out to him, the manager will be most anxious to assist. Do not forget that his hotel exists because of tourists, many of them Americans."

It made a little more sense as he explained it, but I was still a little doubtful.

"In the meantime," Ernesto said, "I have brought you these." Like a magician producing a rabbit from a hat, he brought two objects out of somewhere in the ragged clothes. It took me a full minute to recognize them as my passport and residence visa.

"Where did you get those?" I exclaimed, grabbing them.

"From the room of Señor and Señora Carrasco," he said. "You said that Señora Carrasco had taken them, so I merely went and took them back."

"Ernesto, you are a jewel beyond price."

"And there is now a matter of one thousand and ten pesetas between us," he said.

I laughed. "You shall have them, Ernesto. But I thought you were charging me only five pesetas for the package of cigarettes yesterday."

"Es cierto," he said, "but today I have brought you a second pack." He produced them from his pocket. They were the same brand as he'd given me the day before.

"From the warder again?" I asked.

He shook his head, grinning. "From one of the guards. I think the warder may have suspected me. Today he was careful not to get to close."

The possession of my passport and visa made me feel like a new man. Somehow it gave me more security than the thought that my desire to see the Ambassador was being passed along a chain of command. For the first time I was able to start thinking about something outside of myself. "What's been happening with the Carrascos?" I asked him.

"No hay novedad," he said. "I have not seen the Señora Carrasco since night before last. I think perhaps they had a lovers' quarrel."

"Why do you say that?"

"I did not see her yesterday or this morning, and the Señor Carrasco does not look happy. Maybe she has left him."

I hoped fervently that she hadn't. I knew that she would never leave him before she got her hands on the Tavernier Blue. If she had left, it would be a bad sign.

"Keep on watching them, Ernesto," I said. "As soon as I get out, you'll get your pay."

"It mounts up," he said uncertainly. "But I trust you, Señor. We are truly partners."

"More than ever," I told him, and I meant it.

The warder appeared as a signal the time was up. Ernesto scooted out. I noticed the warder watching him thoughtfully.

"Your nephew," he said as we went back to my cell, "brought you some money?"

"They were not able to spare it yet," I said gravely. "But he did bring me some cigarettes. Would you care for one?" He felt at his own pockets before answering. Then he took the cigarette I offered him and reminded me that I owed him three cigarettes. I paid the debt gladly. I didn't even mind when he motioned for me to step into the cell.

"Señor," I said to him before he could swing the door shut, "I would like to see the commandant, or the officer who questioned me four night ago, at once. Please tell them the matter is most urgent."

"Ahora, ahora," he said. The door clanged shut.

It meant no more than it had before. Nothing was changed. Food was brought and the warder and guards smiled politely at my insistence. They were long accustomed to prisoners who demanded audiences and freedom.

If it had been bad before, my imprisonment was now twice as galling. I had the missing passport and visa; theoretically all I had to do was to display them and I would be out. But first I had to find someone to show them to. I knew better than to flash them on the warder. He, most likely, would have taken them, and that might well have been the last of it.

When I was still no nearer to release on the following day, it was almost too much. That night I spent an hour or more hammering on the cell door. Once a guard shouted at me from somewhere in the corridor, but that was the only response. Finally, exhausted, I gave up and went to sleep.

It was two days after Ernesto had brought my passport that the cell door was once more unlocked at an unusual time. The warder and a guard appeared in the door.

"What now?" I asked. I'd about given up hope that it could mean anything.

The warder ignored my question. "Take him," he said to the guard, "to Capitán Jesús Fernando García."

I didn't have any idea who Capitán García was, but the very title whipped up my drooping hopes. I lit a cigarette and even managed to blow a little smoke in the warder's face as I passed him.

Once more I crossed from the prison to the police building and followed a uniform through the twisting corridors. Back to the same room from which I had started the opposite way.

I realized with a start that that had been only a week before; it seemed like months.

I was soon standing once more across the desk from the hard-eyed young man who had questioned me that first night. He, it turned out, was Capitán García.

"Well," I said, "have you finally gotten around to checking with your own department and learning that I was issued a visa?"

He glanced at his desk, then looked up again. He seemed rather distantly amused. "Señor March, we have not checked anywhere. I merely have been too busy to question you further. But the proof of your innocence lies with you, not us."

The feel of the passport in my pocket added extra ice to my tones. "What is it I have to prove, Capitán? That I have a passport?"

"You were charged with having no passport or visa and having possibly entered Spain illegally."

"Then I demand that you release me," I said. I drew the passport and visa from my pocket and flung them on the desk before him.

He looked startled. He picked them both up and examined them.

"Where did you get these?" he asked.

"The passport from the American State Department and the visa from the Dirección General de Seguridad."

"Of course," he said. "But how did you obtain these in prison? You did not have them when you entered; now you have them."

"I guess they were just temporarily mislaid," I said airily. "Now may I go?"

"I suppose it was the nephew," he said. "I did not learn about that until after the second visit or it would not have been permitted."

I held out my hand. "May I have my passport?"

"Not so fast, Señor March. It would seem to be true that we can no longer charge you with not having a passport, but this matter seems to be very unusual. I think it bears further investigation—unless you care to confess the whole matter right now."

I told him what he could do. While not as blunt as it would have been in English, it was more colorful in Spanish.

"*Estése quieto,*" he shouted angrily. He started to say something else, but the telephone interrupted him. He snatched up the receiver. "*Diga. Quién habla?*"

The expression on his face changed as he listened. Once he glanced quickly at me.

"*Espere un momento,*" he said finally. He held the receiver toward me, his face still tight with anger. "*Le llaman por teléfono, Señor.*"

I took the receiver. "Milo March here," I said.

It was the American Ambassador. He explained that he had just received a phone call from the manager of the Palace Hotel telling him about my predicament. He wanted to know what was happening now.

"I think Capitán García is releasing me," I said. I looked at the Capitán. He had either recovered from his anger or was suppressing it. He nodded when I looked at him.

"Ya lo creo," he said. "You may leave as soon as you've finished your conversation, Señor March."

I repeated what he said to the Ambassador.

"Good," he said. "Call me as soon as you reach your hotel, Mr. March. If I don't hear from you within an hour, I'll get in touch with Capitán García again."

"I'll call you as soon as I reach my hotel," I said, mostly for the benefit of Capitán García. "Thank you, sir." I put the receiver down and looked at him. "Well, Capitán?"

He spread his hands in a graceful gesture. "Your 'nephew' is a very smart boy, Señor March," he said. "It would appear that we have made a small mistake. It is regrettable, but such things happen. You know how it is?"

"I know how it is," I said evenly.

He opened a drawer in his desk and brought out my things. "You have the receipt I gave you?" he asked.

I nodded and produced it.

He checked off the items one by one and handed them to me. When he handed me my money, I made a show of counting it, but even that didn't ruffle his new amiability.

"Everything is here," I said. I put as much surprise in my voice as I could, but he let the insult pass.

"You have our apology, Señor." He smiled at me. "Everything is all right now?"

"Sure. Fine."

"Bueno!" He held out his hand. "America is a great friend of Spain, Señor March. We are always happy to do what we can for Americans."

"Sure," I said. I shook hands with him and worked up

a smile. "No hard feelings." I started to leave, then turned back. "Sorry to bother you, but I wonder if you could show me how to get out of here? I'm afraid I don't remember how we came in."

"Surely," he said. He got up and politely took my arm. We went into the anteroom. There were a number of cops around. The Capitán murmured something to them about the mistake and went through the outer door with me. The several corridors stretched out on either side. They were empty.

"You go down this way, Señor March," he said, pointing. "The first turn to the right, then the next two left turns. That will take you out on the Puerto del Sol."

"*Gracias,*" I said.

He started to turn, smiling. I hit him at the base of the jaw as hard as I could. The smile froze on his face and his legs folded. He slid down the wall to the floor. It was the prettiest sight I'd seen in a long time.

I opened the door to the office and poked my head in. "I am sorry, Señores," I said politely, "but I'm afraid that Capitán García has fainted. He must have been working too hard."

I walked down the corridor with a light step as the cops gathered around him on the floor.

A few minutes later I stepped out into the sunshine. It had never felt so good. I stood there, letting it soak into my face, breathing air that was free of the odor of disinfectants that smothered the prison. I heard my name called. I looked around. It was Ernesto.

"Señor March," he cried, running up, "you are here. The machinery has been in operation."

"The machinery has operated, Ernesto," I said. "Thanks to you. There is a small matter between us, but I owe you far more than that."

"It is nothing, Señor."

I pulled out my money and counted peseta notes into his hand. The fourteen hundred pesetas I owed him. Then I added another six hundred pesetas. Not that I thought the money would repay him for what he had done, but I knew he could use any extra money he got. Great Northern certainly wouldn't miss an extra twelve bucks.

"Señor, you are a *caballero*."

"So are you, Ernesto." I cuffed him lightly on the side of the head. "What about our friends, the Carrascos?"

"He has not left the hotel in three days and I have not seen the Señora."

"Okay, Ernesto. I'll see you later." I walked down the street. I was conscious of not being dressed for an Easter parade. My suit looked like it had been slept in—and it had been. I wore a full week's growth of beard. My shirt was seven days darker than it had been when I went into prison. I would have created quite a sensation in the lobby of the Palace Hotel.

I went into a barbershop. While I was getting a shave, they sent a boy out to get me a new shirt. There wasn't much that could be done about the suit, but it could pass muster. It would have to.

The manager caught sight of me as soon as I entered the lobby. He rushed to meet me, assuring me in a rush of words that my room hadn't been touched while I was gone, that the entire staff was prostrated over my misfortune, and that

I shouldn't judge Spain by the police. He also wanted to be sure that the American Ambassador appreciated his small role in the matter.

In order to reassure him, I called the Ambassador from his desk. I reported that my freedom was now a reality and thanked him again. When I hung up, I told the manager, who was fluttering around me like a wounded bird, that the Ambassador felt eternally indebted to him. The Ambassador hadn't said that, but it made the manager feel so good, I figured it was worth it.

I exchanged a few more compliments with the manager and started for the elevators. Halfway across the lobby I encountered Carrasco. I was startled by the change in his appearance. He seemed strangely withdrawn, as though unaware of the world outside him. If I hadn't stopped him I doubt if he would have seen me at all.

"Don Sansón, how are you?" I asked, grabbing him by the arm.

It took him a full minute to focus his gaze on me. Even then he seemed to be only half seeing me. "Señor March," he said. *"Cómo se encuentra usted?"* He had stopped being friendly with the world. "You have been away?"

"Yes," I said. "And how is Señora Carrasco?"

I thought I'd lost him again. His eyes went blank. Then they struggled back to focus on my face and I could see the pain in them. "Elena has gone," he said.

"I'm sorry," I said. I was. Partly on his account and partly because I was afraid that where Elena had gone the diamond might be. I took a chance on finding out more. "Did she take anything with her?"

"Anything?" he repeated. "Only herself—and my heart." His gaze went blank again. I think he forgot that he had been talking to me. He started on across the lobby in the direction of the patio. I let him go.

I'd have to try again to see if she'd found the diamond, but the first thing I wanted was a shower and a change of clothes. Even the diamond seemed less important than those. It was probably my imagination, but the smell of the prison clung in my nostrils.

The elevator stopped at the sixth floor and I walked down to my room. I unlocked the door and stepped inside. I closed the door and started toward the bathroom, tugging at my coat as I went.

Then I stopped.

Elena Rivelles Carrasco hadn't gone very far, although her going had been permanent. She was sprawled across my bed with her blond hair tumbling over the edge. She wore a blue robe, which was thrown open. There was nothing beneath it. Just under her left breast there was a round black hole. A streak of dried, blackened blood trailed across her ribs.

She must have been dead for at least three days. There was already a faint odor in the room.

TEN

There was no doubt in my mind, even as I first looked at her, what had happened. Samson Carter had indeed come back. Elena must have gotten too close to the big diamond; or she let him discover that it was the diamond which interested her. This was a threat to the world he had built for himself, and he had reacted to it exactly as he had in New York and Lisbon. I could imagine the conflict that must have raged in him. Sansón Carrasco loved her; Samson Carter had to kill her.

There was a bath towel on the floor beside the bed. I picked it up. There was a hole in it and it was heavily burned. He had evidently wrapped it around the gun to muffle the sound of the shot.

The question that bothered me was why had he put her in my room. Was it merely because it was convenient and he knew that I was away, or was there some other reason?

I started to reach for the phone and then pulled my hand back as if it had been hot. I suddenly realized that I didn't dare to report the murder. According to my own testimony, this was the woman who had caused me to spend a week in prison by stealing my passport and calling the cops. She was now dead in my room. An autopsy would prove that she was killed while I was in prison, but I also remembered that I had clouted Capitán García on the jaw. I didn't kid myself about him; he was a tough one and he'd remember that punch for a long time. I could just imagine how happy it would make him to get me on suspicion of murder. He'd see to it that any autopsy report got sidetracked, if not completely lost.

I thought about it some more, but I could see only one solution. Now that I was back, the chambermaids would start coming in again. If I left the body where it was, it would be found within twenty-four hours. If I planted it anywhere else, it would still be found and then Carrasco would be grabbed. I didn't want that either. If the police got him, I'd have no chance of finding the diamond. Besides, I didn't want to see the little guy in the hands of someone like García.

So it looked as if I had to clean it up in less than twenty-four hours and get out before the explosion came.

I said to hell with it for the time being and went in to take my shower. By the time I was again dressed in clean clothes, I began to feel a little more like coping with the problem. But I didn't want to do my coping with Elena's body sharing the room with me. I got up and left. I was careful to lock the door behind me.

Downstairs, I checked first on the patio. Carrasco was there. He was sitting at a table with a glass of untouched wine before him. He wasn't seeing anything. I knew he was pretty well knocked out, but he'd recover. The diamond would bring him back. He'd loved Elena, but the Tavernier Blue was his first love.

I went into the bar and climbed on a stool. I needed something stronger than sherry, so I ordered brandy. I sipped it and tried to think of some way of flushing the diamond into the open.

You know how sometimes you'll see something without quite registering what you see? That's the way it was with me. I saw a man, looking like just another tourist, talking to one of the bartenders. They both looked at me and the bartender nodded. Then the man started to walk toward me. By this time it had registered.

He was a big, beefy man. Maybe in his middle forties. You could tell by his clothes that he was an American. There was a friendly expression on his face, but he walked in an aggressive manner, like he was about to punch somebody in the nose. It reminded me of the way cops walk.

He came up to me. "You Milo March?" he asked. He spoke in English.

"Yeah," I said and waited.

He grinned and held out a meaty hand. "I'm Martinson. Lieutenant. New York Homicide."

I'm never real crazy about cops, and after my experience of the past week I was in a mood where I didn't even like friendly cops. But I tried to match his grin. We shook hands. "I've been expecting you," I said. "When did you get in?"

"This morning. I was told to check with you."

"Have you seen the local cops yet?" I asked him.

"No. I thought I'd see you first."

"Have a drink," I said.

He hesitated but finally settled for a rye. I sipped my brandy and waited. I was going to let him carry the ball until I got some idea where he was heading.

"Carter's here?" he asked.

"He's here. Only here he's known as Sansón Carrasco."

"Gone Spic, huh?"

"That's one way of looking at it," I said. I wasn't going to start fighting with him this soon.

"You're supposed to be looking for this diamond," he said. "You find it yet?"

"No," I admitted.

He finished his rye. "I don't want to stay in this goddam town any longer that I have to. No point just hanging around until he decides to skip again. Where is he?"

"He's around," I said. "The thing is a little complicated."

"What about the dame I hear is with him?"

"That's part of the complication," I said. "One thing, Lieutenant. If I were you, I wouldn't go to the local cops."

"Why not?"

"You want to take him back to New York, don't you?"

"Yeah. What's that got to do with it?"

"Everything," I said. "This boy's liable to get very popular any minute. New York wants him for murder. If they only knew it, the Lisbon cops want him for murder, too."

"Lisbon," he exclaimed. "He killed somebody there?"

"An old guy named Manuel Maria Tristão. The one who gave him his new passport."

He shook his head.

"And," I went on, "as soon as they find out about it—which won't be long now—the Madrid cops will want him, too. He's killed the dame."

"Jesus," he said. He was silent for a minute. "When did he kill his wife?"

"I think three days ago. So far I'm the only one who knows

about it." I went on and told him the rest—about her stealing my passport, the week in prison, and coming back and finding her in my room. I didn't have any trouble holding his attention.

"The only thing that gets me," I said, winding up, "is why he put her body in my room."

"That one's easy," he said. "If the kitchen help knew you'd been arrested, then you can bet that everybody in the hotel knew about it. If anybody was going to start looking for her, the last place in the world they'd look would be your room. All he did was pick the most unlikely place. Didn't you ever notice the way a magician will hide something right under your nose instead of the places you expect him to? Just the way they have to do everything different. Sometimes I think their heads are screwed on in reverse."

For the first time since this case had started, something stirred in my mind. I stared at him while it blossomed.

"What's wrong?" he asked.

"Not a thing, Lieutenant," I said. "I think you just showed more brains than any cop I ever knew. Look, I want you to give me a couple of hours before you do anything."

"Why?"

"I think maybe I can find the diamond. If I can, then maybe we can get him out before the Madrid cops even start looking for him. If nothing else, we can get him to the American Embassy and then fight it out with them from there." I finished my drink and stood up.

"Where do you think the diamond is?" he asked.

"In his room. Do I get the two hours, Lieutenant?"

"Sure," he said. "I'll wait here for you."

"Okay. Wish me luck."

I left the bar. I went by the patio to check on Carrasco. He was still sitting in the same place with the glass of wine in front of him. I went on upstairs.

I walked past my room and stopped in front of 619. The hallway was empty. It took only a minute to pick the lock. I stepped inside and closed the door. The room looked much the same as the last time I had been in it. I went straight to the dresser.

One of the small drawers held Carrasco's gun and the thimbles and golf balls he used for magic. I looked at the gun first. There was still an empty shell under the hammer. I had another idea while I was looking at it. I took the firing pin out of the gun and slipped it in my pocket. Then I put the gun back.

It was the golf balls I was interested in. Sure, I'd gone over them once, but maybe I'd missed something. It was what the guy had said down in the bar. Something about thinking that magicians had their heads screwed on in reverse. It had reminded me that there was such a thing as left-hand threads. Carrasco had been showing some fancy reverse thinking; it would be just like him to use reversed threads.

It was the seventh one. I'd just about given up hope again when I picked up this ball and twisted the top toward me. It moved and I felt the way a Peeping Tom would if he stumbled on Marilyn Monroe's house. I twisted it rapidly and the top half came off. It was merely a shell with reversed screw threads on the inside.

I glanced down at the other half in my hand and got my first look at the Tavernier Blue. It completely filled the golf ball shell. It caught the sunlight streaming in through the window, turned it into blue fire, and threw it into my eyes.

For just a minute I think I understood the men who become possessed by a jewel. For that minute I couldn't tear my gaze away from that diamond. I looked at the shifting blue light and felt that I held a miracle. I touched it and was surprised to find it was cold to the touch.

I'm not sure how long I stood there, caught in the spell of a piece of carbon. Finally I put the top back and screwed it tight. I felt tired and realized that my whole body had been tense while I was staring at the diamond. I slipped the fake golf ball into my pocket and headed for the door.

Once I hit upon it, I realized I should have thought of this long before. The man in the magic store in New York had told me Carter bought three shells when one was all he needed. And the golf ball made a perfect hiding place. He was always fooling with the golf balls—at least until Elena had made him stop—so that he could always keep the diamond close at hand. By constantly doing magic with the golf balls, he made them the least likely object to suspect. It was the Lieutenant's remark about magicians that first made me think of the threads.

I went back to my own room and tried to ignore the body on the bed. It was easier to ignore it than the smell.

I had an idea about Carrasco. I knew he'd fight like hell to keep anyone from getting the diamond, but I was guessing he'd probably fold once it was actually gone. Still, the best thing to do was not to take any chances. If I could penetrate his shell of isolation, maybe I could get him to go to the American Embassy with me on some pretext. Once there, on what was officially American soil, the Lieutenant could arrest him.

I pulled out my suitcase with the idea of packing. There was a knock on the door. While I was debating whether to answer or not, the knock was repeated. There was something frantic about it.

"Who's there?" I called in Spanish.

"Ernesto," came the answer. "Quickly, Señor."

"Come in, Ernesto," I said.

He came in fast, slamming the door behind him. He had his mouth open to say something when he saw the body. His eyes got big and he hurriedly crossed himself.

"Dios mío," he said. "Then it is true. What I just heard."

"What did you hear, Ernesto?" I asked.

That snapped him out of the trance into which the sight of the body had plunged him. "There is no time to lose, Señor," he said. "The police are already on their way up here. I heard them downstairs. And I heard one of them say that you had murdered a lady. The one who was saying it spoke English, but there was one who translated what he said."

"What did he look like?" I asked.

He rattled out a description. It fit the Lieutenant. I cursed to myself.

"Hurry, Señor," Ernesto said.

I looked around the room. There was nothing of mine in it except some clothes and the suitcase. It would be better to leave everything as it was on the hope they might expect me to come back. That would slow them up. I kicked the suit-case under the bed.

"All right, Ernesto," I said. "If they're on their way up, how do we get out?"

He opened the door and looked into the hallway. He nodded and I followed him out. "Down the service elevator," he said. "It is the way I came up. My mother's cousin is waiting below. He will see to it that we get out through the rear entrance."

We hurried down the hallway and turned down an unfamiliar corridor. Back of us, out of sight, I heard the sound of the elevator doors opening. Ernesto heard them, too, and put his finger to his lips in a gesture of silence. He grinned at me, looking more than ever like a little old man.

The service elevator was waiting. We got in and Ernesto punched a button. The door slid shut and the elevator dropped.

A slim youth in a white uniform waited beside the elevator in the basement. It must have been near the food bins, for I could smell the sweet odor of fresh vegetables. Ernesto and I followed the boy back through a dim light.

As we hurried, I was thinking. Ernesto's description had fit Lieutenant Martinson. If that was right, it was the Lieutenant who was bringing the cops after me. It had to be right; except for Carrasco, he was the only person who knew that the girl's body was in my room. He must have gone for the police the minute I went upstairs. I thought back over our conversation, looking for the reason.

It hit me like a ton of bricks. I'd almost been a sucker: without Ernesto I would have been. I consoled myself by thinking that I would have caught it if I hadn't been so concerned with finding the diamond and finding it fast.

He had tipped his hand twice, but I hadn't realized it at the time. The news of the murder in Lisbon had been a surprise to him. It wouldn't have been if he'd been from New York Homicide. John Franklin knew about it and I knew he would give the cops everything he had. But the second slip was an even bigger one. This guy had known that the blonde was married to Carrasco. I hadn't even told Franklin that, so there was no way that the New York cops could have known about it. Lieutenant Martinson was someone else—probably Martin Lomer. Martin Lomer, Lieutenant Martinson.

It fit. Franklin said the blonde rarely worked alone. She had worked once before with Martin Lomer. I knew that Lomer was in Madrid, yet he hadn't shown up on the scene before. He'd been masterminding it from the hotel across the street. Then he hadn't heard from the girl in several days and decided to check up. From the time Elena suspected me, and probably reported to him, he'd had a week to check up on me—the week I'd been in prison. If he were as smart an operator as he was supposed to be, he could easily have found out about me. He might even have known my name in advance; big jewel thieves are apt to keep up on the names of insurance investigators. And he might just as easily have also learned that New York was sending a Homicide dick over. So he'd come along with the intention of pumping me.

I cursed again. Then I grinned. Maybe he'd pumped me, but he had also unwittingly given me the clue that led me to the diamond.

The boy in the white uniform opened a door and we stepped outside.

"Where are we now?" I asked Ernesto.

"Calle de Cervantes," he said. "This way, Señor."

We cut down the Calle de Cervantes until we reached the Calle de Medinaceli. We turned right and that brought us to the Carrera de San Jerónimo.

"Where now, Señor?" Ernesto asked. "The airport and the getaway?" There was the American movie influence again.

"Not yet," I said. I decided to borrow a leaf from Carrasco's book; if it had worked so well for him, it might for me. "To the Puerto del Sol. We'll pick a café right across from the Dirección General de Seguridad."

"Caray!" he said. "You are truly a *caballero,* Señor March." He hesitated, looking at me out of the corner of his eye. "You killed her for sending you to the prison?" he asked.

"I didn't kill her, Ernesto," I said. "She was murdered at least three days ago and put in my room. But it would have been rather difficult to explain it to the police. Especially since this morning, on leaving, I punched a certain Capitán García in the jaw."

"Caray!" he exclaimed again. "This becomes a tale. Do you always live in such adventure, Señor?"

I laughed down at him. "Not always, Ernesto. And the less of it there is, the better I like it."

He shook his head. He did not believe me. Obviously I lived just like Humphrey Bogart in a movie.

We soon arrived at the Puerto del Sol and went to a café across the street. The waiter frowned at the sight of Ernesto but raised no objection when he saw the expression on my face. I ordered a drink for myself and hot chocolate for Ernesto. He perched on the edge of his chair, doing his best to look like a man of the world.

"The first thing," I said to him, "is to check on the line of retreat."

I left him at the table and went back to use the phone. I called the Barajas airport and asked about schedules to New York City. There was a plane leaving for Paris in a little more than two hours, with immediate connections for New York. But there were no available seats. The first plane on which there would be seats was the following day.

On the way back to my table I saw Don Raimundo. He smiled and nodded his head. He was at a table by himself with his usual glass of *tostado* in front of him. I suddenly remembered that Don Raimundo had connections and I felt a little better about the plane situation. Maybe something could still be done.

"Ernesto," I said, arriving back at the table, "I want you to do me a favor."

He gulped the last of his hot chocolate and stood up. "Anything, Señor," he said.

"Go back to the Palace Hotel," I said. "No one there knows of your connection with me, so it won't make any difference if you are spotted. I'm pretty sure you will find Señor Carrasco in the patio of the hotel. Tell him that I want to see him and bring him back here."

"De dos zancadas," he said. "In no time at all." He was off down the street at a run.

I grinned to myself. I was going to try to do something that would disturb the rest of the Board of Directors of Great Northern if they knew about it. They wouldn't like the idea of me hanging around with their seven hundred thousand dollars in my pocket; they would have expected me to say to hell with everything else. But I was going to do my best to get out of Spain with the diamond *and* Carrasco.

I suppose it wouldn't make much difference who arrested Carrasco. He had committed three murders in three different countries. But I knew what would happen to him in Spain. If I took him back to America, at least I could see that he had some help. The American cops would sneer just as much as the Spanish ones at his condition, but I could get hold of the psychiatrist who had once treated him and maybe something could be done.

It wasn't too long before Ernesto was back with Carrasco. He was still as much within his shell as he had been before. But he had come and that was all that counted.

"It is kind of you to want to see me, Señor March," he said. He was still the polite grandee he had imagined himself to be, but I don't think he really knew what he was saying.

"Es algo trivial," I said. I waited until he seated himself at the table. Then I turned to Ernesto. "One more thing," I said. "Do you know a taxi driver named Bernardo? I think his last name was Goma."

He nodded.

"Find him and bring him here," I said.

Ernesto darted away and I turned back to Carrasco. He was staring vacantly into space. I was sure he hadn't heard a word that had been said.

"Señor Carrasco," I said. There was no response. "Or would you rather that I called you Mr. Carter?"

It took a couple of minutes for it to penetrate, but it did. His gaze swung around to meet mine and I could see the awareness struggling to the surface.

"I want to talk to you about the Tavernier Blue," I said.

He was coming back fast. The danger to his fantasy was enough to do it. And I saw something in his eyes that I had never seen there before—the same thing, I was sure, that only three people had seen as their last sight.

"El Tavernier Azul?" he asked softly. It was Samson Carter looking out through his eyes, but he still clung to the Spanish of Sansón Carrasco. "What do you know of it, Señor March?"

"Everything," I said. I wanted to get it all in before he reached the decision toward which he was struggling. "I know everything that you went through to obtain it. I know about the guard in New York, the old man in Lisbon—and Elena. I know that the German I caught in your room was after it. I know that others were after it. I know that is why Elena married you."

"And you are also after it," he said.

"Yes," I said. "But I am after it for the House of Stones and the insurance company. The others—and I don't know how many others—are after it for themselves. They have been after it from the minute that the world learned what you had done."

His lip curled. *"Pon lo tuyo en concejo—"* he began, only to break off. I thought it was something from *Don Quixote,* but I wasn't sure what.*

"I know where the Tavernier Blue is," I said.

The look in his eyes sharpened.

"It is no longer in your room at the hotel, Señor Carrasco," I said quickly. "No longer in the hollow golf ball ... I have it."

He was silent for a heartbeat. "Gone ... ," he said uncertainly. His gaze seemed to turn inward. "Gone ..."

---

* Literally, to submit your affairs to counsel. The line from *Don Quixote* is: *No dirás desto nada á nádie, porque pon lo tuyo en concejo [consejo] y unos dirán que es blanco y otros que es negro.* Don't say anything to anyone, because if you ask advice from other people about your own business, some will say it is white and others will say it is black.

INTERLUDE 5

… He heard it distinctly. A sound within his own head that was not a sound. And with it came a vision—the vision he had struggled so long to see. He had lost the blue diamond; the man who sat across from him now had it. But suddenly he could see the diamond more clearly than he had ever been able to see it when he held it in his own hand. He could see into the very center of the diamond where the blue fire swirled and flickered. As he stared at it with his mind's eye, the flames steadied and he saw what was there in the heart of it.

It was his own face that stared back at him from the center of the Tavernier Blue. He could see it clearly now. He had been imprisoned in it all his life. It was like a revelation. It explained everything in his life.

Now that it was too late, he realized what he should have done. He should have smashed the piece of glass and liberated himself. He should have hammered it until the blue flame was gone. Then he would have been free.

Now it was too late. …

ELEVEN

"Gone ... ," he said again.

When he looked up again, I saw what it was that was gone. I didn't understand what had happened, but I knew that Samson Carter was gone. The man who sat across from me now was Sansón Carrasco—but a different one than Carter had originally imagined. He was older, and in some way he had withdrawn entirely from the world of reality. In some way he reminded me of Don Raimundo.

I was so sure of this impression that I couldn't resist testing it.

"Do you understand that I have the diamond?" I asked in English.

"*No comprendo,*" he said simply. I had the feeling that he had forgotten all the English he ever knew.

"*Escúcheme usted,*" I said. "It will not be long before the police of Madrid will find Elena. I would rather that they didn't get you. The same penalty faces you in America, but I think I can get some help for you there. I am going to try to leave very soon for America, and I want you to go with me."

He smiled at me. "I will do as you suggest, Señor," he said. "You have taken that which is me and I must go where you wish."

It made me shiver. It was obvious that in some way he had

so identified himself with the diamond; his tone implied that I now owned his soul. I wished that I'd never heard of the Tavernier Blue.

Before I could say anything else, Ernesto arrived. "I found Bernardo," he announced proudly. "He is waiting." He gestured toward the street where I could see the taxi.

"I must make arrangements," I said. "You will wait for me, Señor Carrasco?"

"Claro que sí," he said politely.

Ernesto looked at me meaningfully. *"Los pescadores tendieron la red,"* he said. "The fishermen spread out the net."

"I'm sure they do," I said. "I'll be right back."

I went over to the table where Don Raimundo sat. We inquired politely about each other's health and then I asked him if he would do me a favor. He said that he would be delighted. I explained that I and my friend Don Sansón wished to get on the next flight to Paris and that we needed the aid of his *enchufe.* I followed him back to the phone.

Once more he put in his call to Don Estebán. There followed a long and rapid conversation. I gathered that Don Estebán was not at home. Finally, reluctantly, he replaced the receiver and turned to me. I could see lines of embarrassment in his face, but they quickly smoothed out.

"It appears, unfortunately, that my cousin, Don Estebán, has gone to Seville," he said. He appeared to be struggling with thought. "Of course it is my desire to give you all the assistance I can. You are flying to Paris? I imagine that you would like to know if the weather forecast is favorable to flying?"

I got it then. His cousin, Don Esteban, was his only source of *enchufe*. When Don Esteban was not available, Don Raimundo's influence was a thing all shadow and no substance. In his way he wasn't very unlike Carrasco.

"It would be a great help," I said gravely.

I stood by, concealing my impatience, while he telephoned Don Luís Arrese, director of the government weather bureau. Again he went through the business of introducing himself as the cousin of Don Esteban María Paulino y Aranda. More polite conversation and then he brought up the reason for his call. A moment later he informed me that the weather forecast was ideal for flying.

I thanked him and headed back for my table. I saw Ernesto scooting back ahead of me and realized he must have followed to listen.

"What is the trouble, Señor?" he asked me when I arrived at the table.

I explained it to him.

"Señor," he said in wounded tones, "you should know better than to ask those old ones for anything. They are no good for arranging matters of importance. Come. We must hurry to Barajas."

"You can arrange this, too?" I asked in surprise.

"We shall see," he said with the dignity of an adult.

"Shall we go, Señor Carrasco?" I said.

"As you wish, Señor," he said.

We walked out to the cab. Ernesto darted across the street and came back with another boy, smaller and more ragged than himself.

"This," he said, "is Ramón. His uncle works at Barajas. I have told him that you will pay him for his time, Señor."

"Of course," I said.

We all crowded into the taxi and Bernardo got under way.

It lacked only a half hour to flight time when we pulled in to the airport, and I was not feeling optimistic. Ernesto had produced miracles in the past, but there had to be an end to them sometime.

"You wait in the taxi, Señor," Ernesto said. "We will see Ramón's uncle and also make sure that there are no fishermen around."

I grinned at him and leaned back. He had taken charge, but I was quite sure he knew what he was doing.

In ten minutes they were back.

"It is arranged, Señor," Ernesto said triumphantly. "Ramón's uncle works in the ticket office. He will see to it that two other reservations are canceled—they are fat merchants going to Paris for reasons other than business—and you will get them. I have told him that you would give him one thousand pesetas. Was that all right?"

"It was wonderful," I said.

"Hurry," Ernesto said. "There is just time to get through customs and get on the plane."

I had a last-minute fear. I turned to Carrasco. "You have your passport with you?" I asked.

"Of course," he said. He patted the breast pocket of his coat and smiled.

We went first to the ticket window, where I took care of Ramón's uncle and got our tickets. While we were waiting at the customs, I turned again to Ernesto. I still had about five thousand pesetas in my pocket besides my dollars. I was allowed to take two thousand out, but I thought to hell with it. I gave all of it to Ernesto.

"Two hundred pesetas for Ramón," I told him. "Then I want you to do one more thing for me, Ernesto, and you may then keep all that is left."

He nodded and waited to hear what it was.

I wrote down John Franklin's name and address on a slip of paper along with a few more lines and gave it to him. "Send a cablegram to that man," I told him. "Say, *Milo on way back with everything.* And sign it *Ernesto Pujol, assistant to Milo March.*"

His face beamed. "I will do as you say," he said proudly. "Someday, Señor, I will come to America and you and I will be partners again. Truly."

"Ernesto," I said, "you do that and I'll stop working for my boss, and you and I will go into business together. Truly."

It made him happier than the money had.

We were soon through customs and on the plane. A few minutes later it trundled across the field and took to the air. As it lifted from the ground, I looked back. I could see the small, ragged figure still standing there watching the plane. I waved to a *caballero* even though I knew he couldn't see me.

As the plane reached its altitude, Carrasco looked out the window in the direction of the Guadarrama Mountains.

"Nowhere," he said with pride, "is there such beauty as there is in Spain." He sounded as if he'd lived there all his life.

"Are you afraid of going back?" I asked him.

"A Carrasco is never afraid," he said. He looked at me in astonishment. "Why should I have fear, Señor? I have done nothing."

"Nothing," I agreed. I had no intention of reminding him.

He was silent for a minute. "All my life," he said finally. "I have tried merely to live as a man can. But men, Señor, do not live as they once did. It is not as in former ages when there were certain men who took upon themselves the defense of their country, the protection of women, the succor of orphans, the punishment of the proud, and the rewarding of the humble."

It sounded familiar, but I said nothing. After a minute, he spoke again.

"Ya no ay ninguno," he said, *"que saliendo deste bosque entre en aquella montaña, y de alli, pise una esteril y desierta playa del mar, las mas vezes proceloso y alterado; y hallando en ella y en su orilla un pequeño batel sin ramos, vela, mastil, ni xarcia alguna, con intrepido coraçon se arroge en el, entre gandose a las implacables olas del mar profundo, que ya le suben al sielo y ya le baxan al abismo, y el, puestro el pecho a la incontrastable borrasca, quando menos secata, se halla tres mil y mas leguas distante del lugar donde se embarco; y saltando en tierra remota y no conocida le suceden cosas dignas de estar escritas, no en pergaminos, sino en bronces."*

I'd been right about the familiarity. It was Don Quixote bewailing the fact that there were no knights to tread deserted shores beside an angry sea, to come upon a deserted boat and to entrust himself to the stormy waves. Such a one, he was saying, would eventually land on the soil of a remote and unknown land where he would meet adventures worthy of being recorded in bronze rather than upon parchment.

The words were those of Don Quixote, but it was a perfect expression of the driving force behind Samson Carter, alias Sansón Carrasco.

He smiled as though at something he saw in an inward vision. "In last year's nests there are no birds this year," he said. "And now let the notary proceed."

He closed his eyes and in a moment was asleep. He slept like a small child, breathing gently.

I took the golf ball from my pocket and unscrewed the top. I looked in at the bauble that had started all this. I wondered how many others had seen the same thing in the diamond that had been seen by the sleeping man beside me. I remembered Robert Stone telling me how many men had died because of it; now three more had died. To those who still hungered for the Blue Tavernier, this would mean only that it was more valuable.

The light shifted in the diamond and for a moment it seemed that there was something alive in the heart of it, concealed only by the blue flames.

I covered the diamond and looked out the window. The sun was dimmer.

AFTERWORD

The Book or the Movie?

The Man Inside (1954) was the only Milo March novel to be made into a film. It was an English film, screenplay by David Shaw, directed by John Gilling, released in September 1958 in the UK (December in the US). "Trudie" was the theme song, a solo by Joe "Mr. Piano" Henderson that reached number 14 on the UK singles chart in 1958; the sheet music was the number one hit of the year.

Trudie is the character who is trying to find the same stolen diamond that Milo was hired to recover. Competing with professional jewel thieves, she insists she has a legitimate claim to the diamond. Trudie Hall was played by Anita Ekberg, which must have been a major draw, yet the film was not highly praised by critics—"a feeble excuse for a chase melodrama," wrote the *New York Times* reviewer, Howard Thompson.*

Milo March, portrayed by Jack Palance, chases across the globe in a CinemaScope tour of glamorous European locales, which include the actress described by Thompson as "a vista herself." Reviewer Steve Lewis wished the film had been in

---

* https://www.nytimes.com/1959/02/05/archives/screen-the-man-inside-chase-drama-on-view-at-local-theatres.html.

color: "Especially considering who his co-star was, and I don't mean Nigel Patrick. The look that Palance gives Anita Ekberg from the bottom of a rooming-house set of stairs, with her at the top looking down, in the tightest-fitting dress you can imagine—well, maybe you can imagine, and no, while black-and-

white may cut it in some movies, it does not in this one."*

I purchased the DVD from the "Loving the Classics" website and began to watch it with low expectations, but I and my husband both enjoyed the movie very much. The casting of Jack Palance was a big surprise to me. Humphrey Bogart was the actor that Ken Crossen once said he would have liked to portray Milo March (not literally for this film, but in general). William Shatner was also named, though I don't know if that was one of Crossen's ideas.** Wikipedia states that Alan Ladd

---

* "Steve Lewis, Movie Review—*The Man Inside* (1958)" (July 13, 2008), http://mysteryfile.com/blog/?p=691.
** See Dickson Thorpe [pseudonym of Nick Carr], "Will the Real Ken Crossen Please Stand Up?" *The Mystery FANcier,* vol. 1, no. 2 (March 1977), p. 6.

and Victor Mature were earlier choices. And according to the *Los Angeles Times* (October 16, 1957), Gina Lollobrigida was considered for Trudie and the English actor John Mills for "the bad man."

The painter Robert McGinnis used James Coburn as a model for Milo March on the front covers of the Paperback Library series of Crossen novels. McGinnis must have already made many sketches for his Coburn movie posters, so the choice was convenient. It is reported in *The Art of Robert E. McGinnis* that the artist anxiously expected Coburn to object to the use of his likeness, but that never happened.

I agree with Mike Grost's conclusion that Jack Palance "captures Milo March to a T: macho, fun loving, cocky, skeptical, smart, and enjoying traveling. Palance also looks like March, tough, athletic, well-dressed in a corporate executive's suit, smooth, and with lots of energy."* In addition, I like the way Palance captures Milo's quick repartee. For looks, if Milo were portrayed in a film today, I might envision John Hamm in the role.

Another big hit in the movie is the singer Anthony Newley,

---

* mikegrost.com.

who plays Ernesto—not the ten-year-old street urchin of the book, named Ernesto Pujol, but a cab driver whose character lends humor and music to the plot. In the book, the cab driver is named Bernardo Goma. I wonder why they thought Ernesto Garcia was a better name.

The following exchange takes place in Steve Lewis's 1975 interview with Kendell Foster Crossen:

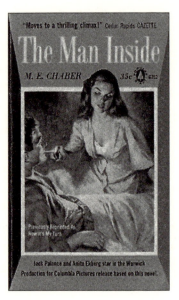

[LEWIS]: How do you obtain the necessary background for the March stories?

CROSSEN: Pure research. I have street maps of almost every major city in the world and have always done a lot of other research on things that would come up in the story. For example, *The Man Inside* took place mostly in Madrid, Spain, and Milo stayed in the Majestic Hotel there. I had a floor plan of the hotel. After the book was out, I had a letter from the Majestic Hotel thanking me for the mention of the hotel and ending with, "And the next time you're in Madrid, please stop in and say hello."*

I wonder if the hotelier's letter arrived after the *movie* came out, rather than the book. If Ken is implying that more guests

---

* The interview was published in a fanzine, *The Mystery Nook*, no. 12 (June 1979). It is reprinted in the back of the Steeger Books edition of *No Grave for March*, the second book in this series.

came to the hotel as a result of *The Man Inside,* I think filmed scenes of a hotel and its surroundings would make a greater impact on viewers than written descriptions in a book.

More to the point, Milo stays at the Palace Hotel in the book, and at the Plaza Hotel in the movie. I had a hard time finding information about a "Majestic Hotel" in Madrid. My search eventually turned up the fact that a Spanish double agent against Nazi Germany took a job as the manager of a Hotel Majestic on Calle de Velázquez, Madrid, in 1939. That agent's name was Juan Pujol. What a bizarre coincidence—the same name as the boy character Ernesto Pujol. But the Calle de Velázquez is not in the vicinity of the Cervantean statues that Milo visits near his hotel in both the book and the movie.*

Back to Trudie. A commenter on the Steve Lewis review said that because of Miss Ekberg he had seen the movie one hundred times. The Columbia Pictures Pressbook is full of photos of Trudie/Anita breathing deeply or leaning over in a

---

* I wouldn't be surprised if this were *not* a coincidence, since Ken's character names, when not ordinary ones like Johnny or Betty, often concealed a private joke, such as a reference to a friend or a fictional character or a humorous Yiddish word. Little Ernesto could have been named for Ernest Hemingway (known as Ernesto in Spain), who hung around Madrid and even favored the Palace Hotel and its bar, which he wrote about in *The Sun Also Rises.*

low-cut dress—as Milo would say, it's like looking down the Grand Canyon, only more fun. The publicity sheet (which I found on eBay) brings back the mid-fifties in all their innocence, with peppy ideas for promotion such as giving out guest tickets for the "most four-letter words" made from the title; placing "telescope in lobby aimed at pose of Miss Ekberg in remote window"; "Ekberg-type girl distributing manila envelopes containing small glass stones, some being actual diamonds"; a concession ad saying: "Satisfy 'The Man Inside' with a Man-Sized Hot Dog!"

The film industry is known for its "happy ending" convention, in which goodness and justice prevail. Trudie actually does make off with the diamond, only to return it when she realizes she's in love with Milo, and he seems to reciprocate (I say "seems" because Milo returns in future books to love and love again). A bit of dialogue in the film establishes that Sam Carter is literally in love with the diamond.* By contrasting the Milo/Trudie affair with the Sam/diamond affair, the film subliminally teaches the audience what true love really is.

In that dialogue, the diamond dealer Robert Stone (played by Gerard Heinz) spells out the meaning of the title: "You see, Mr. March, every man is actually two men: the one the world sees, the other the man inside." This cynical view would have us believe that deep inside, every male is secretly obsessed with possessing some object of lust, whether it's a human being or a rock. In the novel, Robert Stone never says a word about "the man inside"; the phrase doesn't appear anywhere

---

* See the dialogue at https://www.imdb.com/title/tt0051893/characters/nm0416228.

in the book except the title.

There is no secret inner man, which is why I like the book better than the movie. Sure, there's a secret self that emerges when Sam Carter becomes his split-off personality, Sansón Carrasco. But the title of the book refers not to a man hidden inside *a man,* but to the elusive reflection of a face that Carter sees inside *the diamond.* He himself understands eventually that all his life he has sought liberation from mental/emotional imprisonment. Anthony Boucher in the *New York Times* called the book "a fusion of the psychological novel with the hard-boiled detective story." In case readers didn't get the psychological part, the author introduced a psychoanalyst who has included Carter as a case study in a book called *The Empty Ones.*

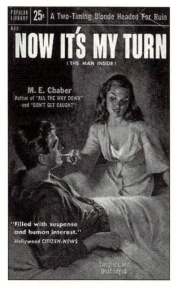

But back to Trudie. I believe a novel and its film adaptation should each be judged on its own merits; yet I can't help contrasting Trudie with her counterpart in the book, Elena Rivelles. Trudie is a sweetheart. Her father was the true owner of the diamond, which was stolen by Nazis during the war. Elena, a gorgeous Spanish woman with dark blond hair, is an international criminal and a cold-hearted seductress. Even Milo has no trouble turning her down when she reveals that her lust for the big blue diamond is greater than her desire for him.

It's unusual that Elena Rivelles is the only woman in the book that Milo makes love with, or almost does. In the majority of the other Milo March books, he goes to bed with at least one or two women, often in a mutually enjoyed romantic manner. When Elena comes to his room, Milo decides he doesn't like the deal she is offering and rejects her despite the desire she arouses. There's no lustful personality hidden inside Milo—it's right there on the outside; it's just not driven and obsessed like Sam Carter's.

In the book, the Tavernier Blue is a fictional gem, said to have been cut from the real diamond of the same name, which was acquired in the mid-seventeenth century by the gem merchant Jean-Baptiste Tavernier.* King Louis XIV bought it and had it cut into the French Blue, which was stolen during the French Revolution. It was recut during this period, and when it resurfaced in 1839 it became known as the Hope Diamond, after the man who owned it. The Hope Diamond was given to the Smithsonian in November 1958 (around the time the movie was released in the UK and America).

The part about the diamond breaking into two, and the larger piece coming into Hitler's possession, is fictional. So the diamond in this novel is not the real Tavernier Blue. But it is true that the real Tavernier Blue and the diamonds cut from it were believed to carry a curse. Why was the diamond

---

* For credible details on the Tavernier Blue, see Mrs. Goddard Orpen, "The French Blue," in *Wide Awake,* vol. BB (Boston: D. Lothrop Co., 1889), pp. 76-80 (free e-book on Google Books, where it is called "volume 28").

in the movie called the "Tyrahna Blue"? To avoid confusion with the real diamond? … *Or was it to avoid the curse?*

Whatever the reason, I am certain that any lingering evil was dispelled from the movie by the angel that was Anita Ekberg.

Kendra Crossen Burroughs

ABOUT THE AUTHOR

Kendell Foster Crossen (1910–1981), the only child of Samuel Richard Crossen and Clo Foster Crossen, was born on a farm outside Albany in Athens County, Ohio—a village of some 550 souls in the year of this birth. His ancestors on his mother's side include the 19th-century songwriter Stephen Collins Foster ("Oh! Susanna"); William

Allen, founder of Allentown, Pennsylvania; and Ebenezer Foster, one of the Minute Men who sprang to arms at the Lexington alarm in April 1775.

Ken went to Rio Grande College on a football scholarship but stayed only one year. "When I was fairly young, I developed the disgusting habit of reading," says Milo March, and it seems Ken Crossen, too, preferred self-education. He loved literature and poetry; favorite authors included Christopher Marlowe and Robert Service. He also enjoyed participant sports and was a semi-pro fighter in the heavyweight class.

He became a practicing magician and had a passion for chess.

After college Ken wrote several one-act plays that were produced in a small Cleveland theater. He worked in steel mills and Fisher Body plants. Then he was employed as an insurance investigator, or "claims adjuster," in Cleveland. But he left the job and returned to the theater, now as a performer: a tumbling clown in the Tom Mix Circus; a comic and carnival barker for a tent show, and an actor in a medicine show.

In 1935, Ken hitchhiked to New York City with a typewriter under his arm, and found work with the WPA Writers' Project, covering cricket for the *New York City Guidebook*. In 1936, he was hired by the Munsey Publishing Company as associate editor of the popular *Detective Fiction Weekly*. The company asked him to come up with a character to compete with The Shadow, and thus was born a unique superhero of pulps, comic books, and radio—The Green Lama, an American mystic trained in Tibetan Buddhism.

Crossen sold his first story, "The Aaron Burr Murder Case," to *Detective Fiction Weekly* in September 1939, but says he didn't begin to make a living from writing till 1941. He tried his hand at publishing true crime magazines, comics, and a picture magazine, without great success, so he set out for Hollywood. From his typewriter flowed hundreds of stories, short novels for magazines, scripts radio, television, and film, nonfiction articles. He delved into science fiction in the 1950s, starting with "Restricted Clientele" (February 1951). His dystopian novels *Year of Consent* and *The Rest Must Die* also appeared in this decade.

In the course of his career Ken Crossen acquired six pseudonyms: Richard Foster, Bennett Barlay, Kent Richards, Clay Richards, Christopher Monig, and M.E. Chaber. The variety was necessary because different publishers wanted to reserve specific bylines for their own publications. Ken based "M.E. Chaber" on the Hebrew word for "author," *mechaber.*

In the early '50s, as M.E. Chaber, Crossen began to write a series of full-length mystery/espionage novels featuring Milo March, an insurance investigator. The first, *Hangman's Harvest,* was published in 1952. In all, there are twenty-two Milo March novels. One, *The Man Inside,* was made into a British film starring Jack Palance.

Most of Ken's characters were private detectives, and Milo was the most popular. Paperback Library reissued twenty-five Crossen titles in 1970–1971, with covers by Robert McGinnis. Twenty were Milo March novels, four featured an insurance investigator named Brian Brett, and one was about CIA agent Kim Locke.

Crossen excelled at producing well-plotted entertainment with fast-moving action. His research skills were a strong asset, back when research meant long hours searching library microfilms and poring over street maps and hotel floorplans. His imagination took him to many international hot spots, although he himself never traveled abroad. Like Milo March, he hated flying ("When you've seen one cloud, you've seen them all").

Ken Crossen was married four times. With his first wife he had three children (Stephen, Karen, Kendra) and with his second a son (David). He lived in New York, Florida, Southern California, Nevada, and other parts of the country. Milo

March moves from Denver to New York City after five books of the series, with an apartment on Perry Street in Greenwich Village; that's where Ken lived, too. His and Milo's favorite watering hole was the Blue Mill Tavern, a short walk from the apartment.

Ken Crossen was a combination of many of the traits of his different male characters: tough, adventuresome, with a taste for gin and shapely women. But perhaps the best observation was made in an obituary written by sci-fi writer Avram Davidson, who described Ken as a fundamentally gentle person who had been buffeted by many winds.

Made in the USA
Middletown, DE
19 July 2020